Judas Pass

Nobody ever crossed Sheriff Chad Cooper – at least not twice. The man was hell on wheels and now the town of Coldwater – his town – was reneging on a bonus of $5,000 they had promised him when he cleaned up the place. Worse still, some of the towns-folk led him into a deadly trap.

But Chad survived and, by Hades, the perpetrators would pay! The trouble was, though, that a bunch of killers on the run was after him. Death stalked him every moment and it seemed that no sooner had he consigned one badman to Boot Hill than another was gunning for him.

His badly scarred and battered frame could surely stand no more punishment but even so he was driven to administer more hot-lead justice. It was a case of kill or be killed.

Judas Pass

JAKE DOUGLAS

A Black Horse Western

ROBERT HALE · LONDON

© Jake Douglas 2001
First published in Great Britain 2001

ISBN 0 7090 7003 9

Robert Hale Limited
Clerkenwell House
Clerkenwell Green
London EC1R 0HT

The right of Jake Douglas to be identified as
author of this work has been asserted by him
in accordance with the Copyright, Designs and
Patents Act 1988.

Typeset by Derek Doyle & Associates, Liverpool.
Printed and bound in Great Britain by
Antony Rowe Limited, Wiltshire.

1
Town Tamer

They watched from the side window of O'Reardon's storeroom as Sheriff Chad Cooper strolled along Main, touching a hand to his hatbrim to folk, inclining his head slightly to the women who smiled at him, some turning to look after him as they passed.

'Popular son of a bitch, ain't he?' opined Mayor Cy Maloney. His mouth was tight and he looked like he wanted to cuss. 'Walks like the town belongs to him.'

'It does in a way, Cy,' O'Reardon said. 'He came in tough and we owe him plenty.'

Maloney turned his head to scowl over his shoulder at the storekeeper. 'Yeah – like the five thousand dollar bonus for makin' the town law-abiding within his twelve months deadline. Which is due to expire in three days. He's already talkin' about the ranch he's aimin' to buy with it. How we gonna come up with that kind of money? That's what this meeting's all about.'

O'Reardon, a short, thick-shouldered man with

pleasant face and a button nose, hitched at his flour-sack apron and looked around at the other two members of the town council: Feeney from the livery and Tennison from Coldwater's biggest saloon, the Waterhole Number One.

'We made the contract, and he'll expect us to stick to it.' He spoke firmly and his eyes were hard as he watched the others. Feeney and the saloon man looked at Mayor Maloney.

The man straightened, taking one final glance out the dusty window as the lawman moved on down the street with that easy-swinging stride they had all come to know so well.

'Town council funds don't run to anywheres near that bonus money, and you all know it,' he said flatly. 'We put on that big Fourth of July celebration this year, rebuilt the church after that trail crew burned it down and so on. Gents, we just don't have that bonus money or anywheres near it.'

'Then that's it,' said Feeney, a hook-nosed, hunched-over man who smelled of horses no matter how many times he washed.

'That's it?' echoed the storekeeper. 'That's *what*, Feeney? That's what you're gonna tell Cooper? We promised him a bonus and he did the job he was s'posed to, made this town's streets safe for our families, and now we can't pay up?'

Feeney shifted his big, straw-fouled boots uneasily.

'Well – *I* don't aim to tell him. That's the mayor's chore. . . .'

'Thanks a lot, you yeller-belly!' growled Maloney, glaring.

'Was *you* wanted that damn Fourth of July thing staged on a grand scale,' snapped O'Reardon bitterly, glaring at Maloney. ' "Extravaganza", for Chrissake! A word you read somewhere and you brought in that circus promoter from New Orleans and told him not to worry about the budget, just to put on the biggest show ever! *That's* why we don't have the bonus money! You just wanted to make sure you'd get re-elected!'

'It worked, didn't it?' snapped the mayor. 'Folk come from all over to see the big parade and them dancin' gals from Morocco and all the rest of it. It put plenty of dollars in the pockets of local business – and, by the by, I don't recollect hearin' you bitchin' none about *that*, Pat O'Reardon!'

'Noooo – I made some money, but that's not what we're talkin' about. It's what we're gonna do about Cooper. He's entitled to that bonus and, God help us, we can't give it to him. Any suggestions, Mayor?'

Maloney curled a lip. 'Matter of fact, yes! We get Cooper's contract from Charley Moseley – he drew it up – and we go over it with a fine-tooth comb and we find some clause in there that gets us off the hook.'

'Why not just tell him we spent the money on the show?' asked Tennison, a quiet-spoken man with a deep voice and a long unsmiling face. 'It's due him, but Cooper ain't the kind of man you can blind-side or feed a load of hogwash. Tell him the truth – that it was spent on the parade. Maybe he'll wait a spell, and we can send him the money in instalments . . .' he almost smiled as he added, 'otherwise, I'm findin' somethin' to do outta town for the next few days.

We've all seen Coop in action. He gets mad and I wouldn't give two cents for this town.'

'What – what's that mean?' stammered Feeney.

'He burned out an entire trail-camp when they wouldn't move to the other side of the river, stampeded their cows to hell, an' gone. He torched Banjo Bella's whorehouse and it was only luck the volunteer firemen saved half of it. He's capable of reducin' this town to ashes if we cross him.'

There was silence in the storeroom and smells of spices and neatsfoot oil and leather and bacon and coffee seemed to close around the men and make the air heavy.

Cy Maloney's mouth tightened. 'Let's check that contract before we start changin' our underwear. There's gotta be some way outta this. I mean, we aimed to stick to the contract, but things just got outta hand. Everyone gripin' that trade was droppin' off because Coop was comin' down so hard on the trail men. We had to do somethin' and puttin' on that big Fourth of July was the answer –' he snapped his gaze at O'Reardon, 'no matter what anyone says.'

O'Reardon nodded, eyes dropping. 'Maybe, Cy, but now it's time to pay the piper . . .'

Tennison heaved to his feet. 'We all knew this was comin' up and we should've done somethin' about it long before now. I'm not makin' excuses, I'm to blame as much as anyone else, but, well, gents, my foreman rode in from my spread last night and says he's ready to go huntin' mustangs. I feel I oughta be there to supervise. . . .'

'You're runnin' out!' hissed Maloney. Tennison

shrugged, adjusted his hat and started for the rear door.

'Could be. Of course,' he added with his hand on the knob, 'we could all chip in – mebbe take up a collection around town. After all, Coop made the place safe for those folk out there. Let 'em pay for the privilege.'

Feeney snorted. 'Don't count on me!'

'You think folk'd give five thousand bucks?' O'Reardon said. 'Not this town – they elected us to hire on a sheriff to clean up this place and that's as far as it goes with them. No, it's our responsibility and, Tenn, you clear town now and you won't be here to vote on any motions this here council comes up with.' He nodded to Feeney and Maloney. 'It'll be two agin one.' He touched his own chest. 'Whatever they want'll go through – it's a foregone conclusion if you go.'

Tennison sighed. 'Sorry, Pat, I just don't aim to underestimate Cooper. I don't say he's greedy, but he's a feller with his own codes who stands by his word and expects others to do the same.' He shook his head. 'We simply can't do it and if we're not puttin' our cards on the table, then I'm out. *Adios*, gents. Lots of luck.'

He went out, closing the door quietly behind him. 'Yeller bastard!' growled Maloney.

'Well, what's it to be?' O'Reardon's voice shook a little; he knew what Maloney was going to say and that the penny-pinching Feeney would back him up.

'We go through that contract with Charley Moseley until we find some way out of it. There *has* to be a way!'

O'Reardon shook his head, but he felt trapped.

He looked around his storeroom, picturing it as a pile of smouldering ash, and shuddered.

He almost wished they'd never hired Cooper to tame the damn town.

It was nearly noon and the men sweating over the contract in O'Reardon's back room were getting nowhere.

Charley Moseley, the lawyer, was a sleek, hawk-faced man in his late twenties. He frowned as he flipped back over the pages of the contract, damp now from their sweaty hands.

He shook his head, pushing back a couple of strands of his dark hair which flopped across his unlined forehead.

'Cy, you asked me to do a good job when I drew up this contract, and I'm proud to say I did a *damn* good job.' He quickly held up a slim hand as the mayor started to scowl. 'I gave you what you wanted. You can't expect me to break something I tried my best to make *un*breakable.'

'Who says I can't?' snapped Maloney, leaning forward aggressively. 'There has to be a way to break it! I know you damn lawyers – you *always* leave your-selves an out. Now you show us where it is!'

Moseley wasn't exactly afraid of the mayor but he knew the man was vindictive, even violent at times; he could affect his business if he got on the wrong side of him. He hesitated, then said slowly, 'There is one aspect that could be used – but I doubt you'd be able to arrange it. . . .'

Feeney and Maloney were all ears and expectations.

'I put in a clause that said if Cooper's actions endangered the town or its inhabitants in any way then the contract could be terminated immediately.'

'What in hell does that mean?' growled the mayor.

Charley waved airily. 'It's just one of those . . . precautionary clauses that no one expects to have to use because they're so hard to implement – but it's there. And that's *all* that's there that might allow you to cancel Coop's contract. If he endangers the town, you've got him.'

Fenney looked puzzled. 'Don't sound like much to me.'

Maloney scowled. 'Me, neither.'

Charley shook his head, standing abruptly. 'Well, that's all the help I can give you, gents. Now I'll be going. . . .'

Neither councillor said goodbye and Charley Moseley left in a huff.

After a while Cy Maloney screwed up the contract angrily. He was pale, obviously worried.

'Judas, Feen, what the hell're we gonna do? I sure don't take to the idea of tellin' Coop we can't pay him.'

'Have to offer it to him in instalments like Tennison suggested.'

Maloney gave him a scathing look then sighed. 'Well – I guess that's just what we're gonna have to do.'

O'Reardon, who had been serving in his store, came hurrying in.

'I saw Charley leave – any solution?'

But one look at their faces gave him his answer.

'*Oh, Christ*!' he breathed.

An hour later the telegraph message arrived.

Hap Marcus, the telegraph operator, brought the message to Cy Maloney's office; he had been instructed to deliver any message to do with the town in general, or the law in particular, directly to the mayor. Marcus stood waiting while Maloney snatched the paper and smoothed it out, trying to read the scrawled writing.

> Cal McPherson escaped prison three nights ago. Possibly heading your town. Armed and dangerous.
>
> Kennedy, US Marshal, Denver.

'Ain't that McPherson the feller Coop sent up to Canyon City pen, Cy?' the telegraph operator asked. 'The one swore he'd kill Coop if it took him the rest of his life?'

' 'Course it's the same one!' growled Maloney, studying the paper. 'I just hope the son of a bitch don't come here lookin' for Coop. . . .'

His voice trailed off and he snapped his head up quickly.

'Hap – it's been a long time since you an' me've had a drink together . . .'

Hap blinked. 'We ain't *never* had a drink together, Cy!'

'Well, it's time we did.' Maloney smiled and put

the telegraph message in his pocket. He clapped an arm about the puzzled operator's thin shoulders. 'Let's you and me go have a few, eh? I'm buyin'.'

Hap Marcus frowned. 'Wait a minute, Cy – this ain't like you. And I got my shift to finish . . .'

'Don't worry – I'll fix it with Western Union. Speakin' of which, you an' me'll just kind of keep that message to ourselves, eh? Don't tell no one – not even Coop.'

Marcus baulked at the door. 'But – he oughta know!'

Cy grinned tightly. 'No he don't, Cy. No, he don't oughta know. Now let's go tie one on. . .'

2
Hard to Kill

Chad Cooper was a tall lean man who, many folk claimed, reminded them somehow of a strip of rawhide. Maybe that was because he was rawhide tough, a man who saw a job through to the finish once he took it on. If he trod on toes, hurt feelings, had to use violence, it was all the same to Sheriff Chad Cooper – Coop, most people called him.

His contract with the Coldwater town council was drawing to a close and he was looking forward to it. It had been a tight deal right from the start, signing his name to a paper that guaranteed he would tame this wide-open lawless town and have it up and running as a fine example of law and order within one year.

But Cooper liked challenges, the tougher the better. Besides, they had offered him an extra incentive: $5,000 bonus if he achieved his goal within the time of the contract. It hadn't been easy and Cooper had the scars to prove it. Two bullet holes in his back, a long ridged tear across his lower right ribs, a ragged knife scar slantwise across his chest and he had lost count of the times his nose had been busted. Scar tissue around the eyes and the calloused knuckles didn't bother him – he had earned most of those long before he had ever heard of Coldwater.

Men had ambushed him, waylaid him, tried to con him, ganged up on him and beat the living daylights out of him, certain sure that after recovery Chad Cooper would pull up stakes. *Wrong!* Once he had recovered he went hunting the men who had done these things to him. He tracked them down – and punished – every one. Or allowed the law to carry out the punishment. If it didn't seem adequate, Coop delivered his own justice. After a while the townsfolk got the message: Cooper was going to bring law and order to Coldwater or die trying – and they already knew he was a hard man to kill. So the lawless elements began to give the town a wide berth and the word spread along the trail: *Watch your step in Coldwater. The sheriff's a mean one and rawhide tough.*

The profits in certain businesses dropped off when Cooper enforced the strict new town ordinance he had helped draft. Resentment against him increased at first but no one made any real effort to get rid of him. He was simply too damn tough for them to handle, and then the families and legitimate business folk began to realize just how safe the town had become for them. They could walk the streets without being accosted by drunks or shot at by crazy cowpokes half-mad with rotgut. Their women could walk to church and back in the evening without heavy escorts. Their kids could play safely. The town was peaceful and those loco enough to break the law paid for it. No favourites. No slipping a couple of dollars under the table and getting a light sentence. Those who tried it found themselves up on additional charges of bribery or corruption. Coop faced them all fearlessly.

Suddenly, Chad Cooper was a mighty popular man in Coldwater. And he had enjoyed that popularity and knew he would miss some of the folk in this town when his contract ended and he moved on. But not to another town-taming job. No, sir. He'd had a belly-ful of that, hiring out his gun, risking his neck every time he stepped out on to the street.

No, this time he would collect his $5,000 bonus and he would go looking for a piece of ranchland out along the Mogollon Rim – the 'Muggyown' as the locals called it – and settle down. Maybe there would be a woman he could share his life with, maybe not. He didn't feel quite ready for married life yet – who could tell what might happen. . . ?

He had always liked ranching, had, in fact, spent years as a cowhand, twice as a foreman. He had a natural gunspeed and he could use his fists, knew wilderness lore, and wasn't afraid to crack a few heads if it was needed. He didn't seem to be saving much from his cowboy wages, so when a local sheriff asked him to be his temporary deputy in Wichita, Kansas, he had jumped at the chance. The money was better than punching cows so he had hired out his gun to other lawmen. But that had been the best part of twenty years back and now he would turn forty next April and he figured it was time to think about settling down.

He had worked damned hard for this town and figured he had more than earned the bonus they had promised him.

It was after supper and dark but the extra street lights he had made the Main Street businessmen install outside their premises illuminated the area tolerably well. There were still pools of deep shadow but now folk no longer gave them as wide a berth as they used to. They knew now there was little chance of some would-be rapist or robber lurking there as in the bad old days. Chad Cooper had seen to that.

And he checked out each shadow area as he patrolled the town, occasionally stopping to talk to folk who greeted him, always polite, never seeming to be in a hurry, but his eyes were restless and there wasn't much that Cooper missed.

He had a drink in Waterhole Number One and when he asked for Tennison the barkeep told him the man had had to go out to his ranch on business and wouldn't be back for a couple of days.

Cooper moved on, looked in on the livery, casually checking the horses of new arrivals, making sure none of the brands matched his lists of stolen animals. He glimpsed Feeney in the office and walked down the aisle. He didn't care for the man but he usually passed a little time with him.

'What's your hurry, Feen?' he asked as the livery man started out the rear door of the office.

Feeney snapped his head up, gave a kind of sickly

crooked grin and nodded jerkily. 'Ate too much of the wife's chili, Coop – have to run!'

He grimaced, slammed the door and Cooper smiled as he heard the man running up the well-beaten path to the privy.

He left the livery and checked the doors of a couple of business premises that were closed for the night, then turned into O'Reardon's General Store. O'Reardon himself was behind the counter, weighing up one- and two-pound bags of flour from a cask, liberally spattered with the white stuff.

Somehow he had the feeling that O'Reardon wasn't all that pleased to see him.

'Need some tobacco and papers, Pat.' Cooper brought out come coins and spread them on the counter as the storekeeper dusted off his hands and went to collect the linen sack of Bull Durham and the blue pack of Wheatstraw papers. He added a small carton of vestas free of charge. As he paid, Cooper studied the man closely. 'You feeling poorly, Pat?'

'Me? No!' O'Reardon realized he had been too emphatic and forced a grin. 'Just the flour makin' me look kinda pasty-faced, I guess.'

Coop grunted and began to make a cigarette. O'Reardon stood there, looking uncomfortable, impatient. 'Hear Tenn's out at his ranch for a couple of days. Guess the regular Saturday night poker game won't be on tomorrow, eh?'

O'Reardon shrugged. 'Well, I won't mind – can't really afford to lose any money.'

Cooper looked at him sharply as he fired up his

cigarette. 'Hell, we only play for cents a hand. Business can't be that bad.'

O'Reardon took a deep breath. 'Well, I'll tell you, Coop – it's bad enough so I can't really spend the time standin' here chewin' the fat instead of gettin' on with my chores.' He coloured and looked away from the sheriff's weathered, hard face. 'Sorry, Coop. . . .'

'Don't worry about it. See you some other time.' The sheriff nodded and strolled out. He looked back through the display window, saw O'Reardon back at the flour barrel, cussing a blue streak as his shaking hand spilled a scoopful. 'Mebbe my breath's bad,' Cooper allowed as he walked on down the street.

He was passing the entrance to an alley that ran down beside one of the town's smaller saloons, the Drovers' Place, when he thought he heard a moan. Instinctively, he dropped a hand to the butt of his holstered sixgun, turned into the darkness, back against the wall of the saloon, moving down slowly. It was like walking on the inside of a filled-in grave. No light penetrated and he jumped as his sliding boot kicked a couple of empty bottles together. He dropped to one knee, the gun whispering out of leather, hammer spur drawn back under his thumb.

Nothing happened. Except he heard the groan again. Louder. More pain-filled.

Cooper tightened his grip on his gun.

He'd only travelled a few more feet when he tripped over a body. Down on one knee, eyes straining into the darkness, Chad Cooper waited, left hand groping, feeling a torn and wet shirt beneath his fingers. The wetness had the sticky consistency of blood. His fingertips examined a battered and smashed face.

Or what was left of it. . . .

He fumbled out a vesta and snapped it into flame on his thumbnail, holding it at arm's length away from his body, the gun coming up, searching for danger. No one shot at him or threw a knife. There just seemed to be him and the injured man.

He looked down, wiped some of the blood away from the battered features, bringing fresh groans to the man's split lips.

Cooper could just about recognize Hap Marcus, the telegraph operator. It looked like someone had tried to kick the poor devil to death.

Doc Peebles came out of the infirmary, wiping bloody hands on a stained cloth. He was middle aged, wore pebble eye-glasses on the end of his nose and squinted now at the lawman.

'Not sure he's going to make it, Coop. He's had a really savage beating. Spleen could be ruptured. He's got concussion at least, possibly a fractured skull. Ribs are caved in and he'll be lucky if one of them hasn't penetrated a lung. What was it? Robbery?'

'Don't rightly know, Doc,' Cooper said soberly. 'He had nothing in his pockets but I doubt he'd have been carrying much money. Smelled of liquor. Mebbe he was drinking in the Drovers' and spoke outta turn. I'll look in later, Doc.'

Cooper left and went straight to the noisy, crowded bar of the Drovers' Place. He wasn't all that popular there because he had closed down some gambling tables that he knew to be fixed and he'd made sure the owner, Keno Moran, had been heavily fined. He had also made Keno clean up the dance-hall girl side of the business and to quit watering his liquor. Coop put the lid on the high-jinks Keno used to allow the trail wolves to get away with, too, and that really made him a whole new bunch of enemies.

Cooper lost no sleep over it.

There had been talk, too, that Keno bought running-ironed cattle from some of the rougher trailmen but Cooper had been unable to prove this or he would have closed down the Drovers' completely. Still, he had warned Moran plainly enough: *Cut your connections to the hardcase element, Keno, or I'll run you out of town – maybe ahead of a bullet.*

Keno didn't take to being threatened.

But now he greeted Cooper with a beaming smile as he came out from behind one end of the bar, silk, flowered vest glinting in the lamplight, a long cigar stuck between his thick lips. He always reminded Cooper of a toad, with his wide mouth and permanently squinted eyes, hair brushed flat to his scalp above a high forehead.

'Hey, ain't often we see you in here, Coop. Have a whiskey on the house? Sort of a farewell drink. . . ?'

The sheriff studied the man soberly, noting that the talk and noise in the bar was diminishing rapidly, like a tide going out. He looked around, saw the way the hard-eyed drinkers were watching him – as if they were waiting for something to happen. They were tough *hombres* in this bar. None of them cared much for Cooper, resenting his enforcing the laws that restricted their idea of 'fun'.

A few had tried their luck at squaring things with Cooper, but most were dead now. . . .

'I'll pass on the rotgut, Keno. I found Hap Marcus near beat to death in your alley a while back. He smelled of booze. Who was he drinking with?'

Keno Moran shrugged his shoulders expansively. 'He weren't drinkin' in here.' He looked around at the staring crowd. 'None of you boys seen ol' Hap Marcus in here this evenin', did you?'

The chorus of "no's" rang from the rafters and Cooper knew right away they were lying. But this crew were also grinning. Cooper didn't like that. There was something very wrong here. They were expecting something to happen. . . .

He stepped back, trying to find a clear spot, but realized that the crowd had moved in, cramping him. He was jostled. His gun arm couldn't draw his pistol. Then rough hands gripped him and held him. Keno, still grinning, stepped back and said,

'Friend of yours has been waitin' to see you, Coop.' The man sounded happy as he gestured vaguely above him and Cooper automatically glanced towards the head of the stairs.

He felt his belly knot tight as he recognized the squat figure of Cal McPherson, a rapist and woman-beater he had seen thrown in jail on a ten-year sentence.

McPherson was unsmiling as he shook off the attentions of two of Keno's painted hostesses, slapping one brutally, before starting down the stairs, never taking his bullet-like eyes off the lawman. He was wearing a twin-gun rig, the big Colts dragging at his rolling hips.

'Must be good grub in Canyon City,' Cooper said steadily as the man approached. 'You've put on weight, Cal. You're fat and sloppy as a mud-wallowing hog.'

Every eye in the room turned to McPherson as he stopped dead in his tracks. His moon face seemed to crack, lines writhing across it as he screwed it up. At the same time a blood-chilling whine came from between his thin lips.

Keno laughed quietly, but uneasily, jabbing his cigar towards Cooper. 'You really done it this time, Coop! Cal'll kill you reee-all slow for that. . . .'

Suddenly a fist smashed into Cooper's kidneys and he staggered forward, but was pulled back hard by iron grips on his arms. A raised knee caught him in the same place as the fist; and his legs buckled and he started to fall.

'Hold him!' snapped Cal McPherson, starting forward. 'Hold the son of a bitch!' His voice was womanish but the crazy edge was plain to hear. Men had stepped away from Cooper, except for two. Through the red haze of pain as he sagged in their grip, the sheriff recognized two of McPherson's old bunch. One man he knew only as Spud, and the second, a wanted killer nicknamed 'Bowie' because he liked to chop up his victims with a huge version of the famous *Iron Mistress* carried by Big Jim Bowie. He was fumbling at his belt now so as to free the blade from its sheath.

McPherson stopped in front of Cooper and kicked
him in the midriff. He held out a pudgy hand that
was surprisingly pink and uncalloused, despite the
judge's verdict stating that he was to serve his
sentence with hard labour. He snapped his fingers
impatiently at Bowie.

'Gimme, while I cut the bastard's nose off . . .'

'Aw, Cal, I wanted to do that!' whined Bowie but
McPherson scowled and snatched the heavy, foot-
long blade. 'He's got plenty other parts you can cut
off him,' McPherson said, testing the wide blade's
edge lightly with his thumb. 'Man could shave with
this. . . .'

He lifted the knife towards the sheriff's sagging
head and Keno Moran, looking concerned now, said,
'Cal – hang on! Take this someplace else, huh? A
gunfight I don't mind, but I won't have my bar
turned into a slaughterhouse . . .'

'No?' queried McPherson in his woman's voice.
He slashed backwards, the blade slicing across the
gambler's neck, hacking open a great gash that
spurted blood half-way across the room. Men scattered hurriedly.

Dance-hall girls screamed and some men paled,
many turning to get out of there. And while the
jostling and shoving was going on, Chad Cooper
came to his feet, palming up a hidden derringer
from his boot-top, shoving the barrels into Spud's
face and blasting him back a couple of feet. A large
black hole appeared between the man's eyes.

But he fumbled when switching to the second
barrel, He flung the weapon at Bowie, and spun

towards McPherson as the man grunted and came in swinging the large knife. Cooper caught the killer's arm, surprised at the strength in it, but he bared his teeth, turned the man's wrist so that the blade twisted towards Cal and shoved hard. The point of the blade penetrated McPherson's chest an inch or so and the man's eyes widened as he stiffened, staring into Cooper's stony face. Chad Cooper stared back coldly and lifted his left fist, smashed the heel of the hand down on the knife's pommel as he gripped it in his right hand and McPherson's high-pitched scream was cut short as the blade drove in to the hilt.

Cooper let the dead man fall and twisted towards Bowie who had his Colt out and was cocking the hammer. The killer bared his teeth, knowing he had Cooper dead to rights.

But Chad Cooper's Colt blurred out of leather, As the barrel angled up it roared and a foot of flame reached out to touch Bowie even as the bullet took the man in the chest. A second bullet made sure of him before he stretched out on the floor.

Cy Maloney was mighty nervous, even though he was backed up by O'Reardon and Feeney in his office. They all stared at Chad Cooper in the morning sunlight that streamed through the dusty glass of the single window in the mayor's second-floor office, well aware of the fracas that had taken place in the Drovers' saloon last night.

'Jesus, Coop!' Maloney said abruptly, his voice sounding hoarse. 'Four dead men and they reckon they're still swampin' out the blood!'

'Mostly Keno Moran's,' Cooper said without inflexion. 'Cal slashed his throat.'

Feeney looked like he would be sick.

Coop's gaze made Cy Maloney squirm. 'He's no loss. I've suspected for some time that he's been hiding out men on the dodge. What'd you fellers want to see me about?'

'Cy has somethin' to say, Coop,' said O'Reardon, not looking at the mayor or the liveryman. 'This is none of my doing and I don't go along with it, but as a council member I have to be here. Tennison should be here, too, but I don't reckon he'll show. He's too scared of you.'

That brought a frown to Cooper's face. 'Me. . . ?' He turned his puzzled gaze on to the mayor. 'What is this, Cy?'

Maloney did a heap of stumbling and hemming and hawing and finally Cooper slapped an open hand down hard on the man's desk and told him to 'For Chrissakes, spit it out, Cy, or I swear I'll throw you through that window!'

Maloney blurted it out then. 'You endangered this town's citizens last night, tackling three known outlaws in a crowded bar! Now that's in direct breach of your contract! It clearly states that you are to apply the law when it's needed, and in whatever manner you deem necessary – *so long as it doesn't endanger any citizen of Coldwater!* Now, as I said, you breached that clause last night.'

'You wanted me to stand still and have my throat cut? Wanted me to clear the bar of them hardcases before I fought back?'

Maloney shook his head. 'Of course not, Coop.' The man was gaining more confidence now. 'We know you have to act as you see fit, but – *four dead men* and in a crowded bar! I mean, that's over the odds, you have to agree!'

Coop looked around at all three. 'No, I don't agree,' he said quietly. 'I was set up. But let's get to the real point. Twice you've mentioned that I'm in breach of my contract . . .'

'Charley Moseley will back me up in this!' Maloney said quickly.

'. . . And I got a hunch that you're gonna tell me something I don't want to hear.'

Maloney was by himself now, he saw that with one sweeping glance at Feeney and O'Reardon. The latter had never been with him, of course, but . . . Well, best get it over with!

'What we're tryin' to tell you, Coop, is that because of what you done last night, you just made yourself ineligible for that bonus money.'

The silence sat in that room like a crippled cougar; heavy, still, yet deadly. . . .

It was a long time before Cooper slid his bleak gaze from Cy Maloney's face to Feeney's yellowish features, and on to O'Reardon, who looked sick, sweating.

'I was out-voted, Coop! If Tennison had stayed we'd have had a stalemate but . . .'

'I kind of suspected something was wrong,' Cooper said quietly. 'Knew that big Fourth of July had cost a helluva lot more than you said. I've been trying to get out of Banker Neilsen just how much was in the council funds account but he wouldn't tell me.' He leaned against the wall and slowly shook his head, running his tongue around inside his lower lip. 'So – this is the thanks I get for giving you a safe town . . .'

'Aw, Coop, we didn' want it this way,' moaned Feeney but clamped his teeth together at the look the lawman threw his way.

'You miserable sons of bitches,' Cooper said flatly, straightening, and all three men jumped, pressed back against the wall behind Maloney's desk. Cooper hooked his thumb in his gun-belt and Maloney winced, threw an arm up across his face. '*Miserable!*' Cooper repeated. He walked across and stood in front of each man, glaring coldly down into their frightened faces, for he was inches taller than any of them.

Feeney actually lost control of his bladder. O'Reardon tried to speak but his mouth was too dry. Maloney swallowed and stared with his eyes popping out of his head.

Cooper slapped each man savagely across the face, rocking them on their feet and leaving the imprint of his fingers on their cheeks, then turned and walked out, saying,

'I'll be wanting my pound of flesh.'

3
Cooper's Justice

Cooper was packing his warbag when the doctor sent word that Hap Marcus had died.

'Say anything, Doc?' Coop asked when he went around to see the medic.

'As a matter of fact, yes.' The doctor looked steadily at Cooper and said, 'The only words he managed to gasp were "Message for Coop". He made quite an effort so I put some faith in those words, Coop. He wanted you to know.'

'What was the message?'

'That was all he said. Could he have meant there was a message for you come in on the telegraph?'

'Could be. He had nothing on him when I found him. I'll go see the other operator.'

The man's name was Jensen and he was annoyed that Marcus hadn't finished his shift last night and, because the man was hurt, he had had to stand in for him that morning.

'My wife's birthday of all times and she is not amused.'

'Jensen, Hap's dead. He was beaten to death. Now quit your griping and check your files. Hap would've logged any message that came in.'

Jensen was still tight-lipped but did as Cooper ordered. He looked a little surprised when he found a copy of the message from the Sheriff of Denver. It had been logged at 4.00 p.m. the previous day.

'Should've been delivered to you, Sheriff,' Jensen said haughtily. 'But then again . . .' He clamped his teeth together abruptly, looked slightly alarmed.

'Finish what you were going to say.'

'No – it – it was nothing. I . . .'

'Finish it!' Cooper snapped and Jensen cleared his throat, nodded, and said,

'Well, we'd been instructed that any message that had to do with the town, no matter who it was addressed to, had to be shown to the mayor first.'

Cooper swore softly. 'How long has this been going on?'

'It's standin' orders – from Mayor Maloney.'

'So Marcus would've shown this message about McPherson coming here to the mayor . . .'

'And no doubt he would have passed it on to you.'

Cooper's face was hard as he said, 'Oh, there's a doubt all right. A damn big one!'

He left the telegraph shack and strode back up town to the mayor's office, stopping off briefly at the Drovers' saloon on the way. Maloney jumped when Cooper came in.

'Going someplace, Cy?' Cooper gestured to the

cardboard boxes that were crammed with many of the mayor's belongings from his office.

'I – er – just rearrangin' things, Coop.'

'Uh-huh. Like you rearranged the telegraph operators' orders to show you all messages first.'

Maloney paled. 'Only those that might affect the town! Hell, I'm responsible and . . .'

'Federal offence, Cy. Intercepting US Mail.'

Maloney smiled crookedly. 'It's a private deal – run by Western Union.'

Cooper soon wiped the smile off his face. 'Western Union has Federal contracts, Cy. You're in trouble. But not as much as the other thing.'

Maloney stiffened. 'What – other – thing?'

'The murder of Hap Marcus.'

Maloney sat down, blinking, blowing out his cheeks. 'What're you talkin' about?'

'The men who drink at the Drovers' still don't like me, Cy, but they saw what happened last night in the bar and decided to co-operate today. Said you were in the bar with Hap Marcus, poured the booze into him, got him drunk. You said you'd see him home. Couple hours later I found him dying in the saloon alley.'

'I tried to see him home,' Maloney admitted but his tone told Cooper he had rehearsed this moment in his mind, knowing it must come sooner or later. 'But he was too drunk and wanted to fight so I said to hell with it and shoved him away. I walked on and when I looked back before I turned the corner, I saw him staggering into the alley. Someone must've jumped him in there. But he was definitely all right when I left him.'

'You got him drunk to keep him from telling me about that message from Santa Fe. You *wanted* McPherson to come here, knew he was after my hide, and you figured a loco killer like Cal would brace me right there in the bar. Guess you didn't care who won, because either way you wouldn't have to pay me that bonus.'

Cooper was surprised when Maloney collapsed into his chair, put his head in his hands and began to weep.

'I never meant it to turn out like it did! I never wanted to hurt Hap, just get him fallin'-down drunk so he'd have a helluva hangover and it – well, I hoped your meetin' with McPherson would all be over by then and he'd figure it wouldn't matter he hadn't told you about the message.' He looked up, face deep red, wet with his tears. 'I – I lost control! I'd been so damn worried about that money and how I . . . I – simply lost control! I do, sometimes and . . .'

'Yeah, Cy, I know how worried you'd be . . . But you killed Hap – and you'll pay for it.'

Maloney stared in disbelief, then stood up, swaying. 'You – you ain't sheriff any more, Coop! Soon as you breached your contract last night you lost all your authority! You can't do nothin' to me.'

Cooper smiled thinly and Maloney's face lost all its colour as the ex-lawman walked around the desk, Maloney starting to back away. Cooper reached for his shirt-front, grabbed a handful of cloth and spun him around roughly, changing his grip to the back of the collar and the belt.

Then, still without saying anything, he ran the now

screaming Maloney straight at the window. Maloney's thrashing arms came up to cover his face as he smashed through the flimsy wood of the frame, glass shattering as his thick body hurtled out and went flailing down into the street two storeys below. He hit hard and soddenly and lay face down, unmoving, bloody. . . .

Cooper looked down through the broken window as folk came a-running. 'You're right, Cy. I have no authority here now. All I can do is dish out justice the way I see it. And that's your lot, you two-timing son of a bitch.'

Cy Maloney was going to spend a lot of time on crutches and in a plaster cast. The doctor made a point of telling him that he would expect payment every Saturday – or treatment would not continue.

With his jaw wired shut and his head swathed in bandages, the ex-mayor could do nothing but make growling noises, but arrangements were made through Banker Neilsen for the doctor's weekly payment. (While he was in the infirmary, Mrs Maloney and their only daughter sold the house and took the first train east – no one ever heard of them again.)

The town's conscience was badly pricked and O'Reardon and Tennison started a collection amongst the townsfolk who knew they owed Cooper plenty. They managed to raise almost $700 and while Cooper was grateful, he told them to donate it to Hap Marcus's widow.

Then he went to the livery and roped two fine

horses – a buckskin and a palomino, both geldings – in Feeney's corrals. The liveryman licked his lips and stammered.

'Two most expensive hosses I got, Coop.'

'Yeah, I know. Still won't make up your share of my bonus but they'll do. I'll expect you to throw in pack-saddles and panniers.'

Feeney's jaw dropped. 'You – what? Listen, you can't do that! That's – stealin'!'

Cooper nodded, stroking the palomino's muzzle. 'Well, I guess you'd know stealing if it jumped up and bit you, Feen. Give both hosses a good rub down and curry-combing, and get those pack frames and saddles ready. I'll be back.'

Feeney, almost physically sick, just stood there and watched the man walk out through the big doorway into the watery sun of Main. There were thunder-heads building over the Coffeepots in the north, a sure sign of rain coming.

O'Reardon was offended when Cooper refused to pay for all the supplies he had ordered, including a new model Winchester rifle and ten cartons of .44/40 ammunition. The storekeeper, who had been tallying up the cost as Cooper chose his goods, blinked when the man tore up the bill.

'What's this, Coop?'

Cooper gestured to the large pile of food and ammunition on the counter. He picked up the rifle and began thumbing shiny new cartridges through the loading gate. O'Reardon held his breath. Cooper's eyes were colder than the grey lead of the bullets he fed the rifle.

'Part of your share, Pat. You know what I mean.'

'Judas, man, I stuck up for you! Wouldn't vote with the others!'

'But you didn't give me any warning, Pat. You let me risk my neck, dodging bullets and fists, and didn't bother to tell me I wouldn't be getting that bonus.'

O'Reardon curled a lip. 'You're just a hired gun, aren't you? Nothin' more.'

'That's what I am, Pat – I lay my life on the line for cash.'

There was another customer, a well-dressed medium-sized man who was selecting some bacon and trail coffee and beans. He looked to be in his forties and now turned and looked at the store-keeper and the ex-sheriff, frowning slightly.

'And sometimes I don't get paid,' Cooper added. 'So I take it out in kind. Pack that stuff so I can tote it easily in panniers, Pat. Okay?'

O'Reardon was angry but he wasn't about to argue further with Cooper. As the man swung away towards the street door, new rifle over his shoulder, O'Reardon couldn't resist one last jibe.

'You're a tough man, Coop. But one day maybe you'll find cash ain't enough to pay for your gun. Maybe it'll cost you your life!'

'That's the chance I take, Pat. Be back in an hour.'

The well-dressed customer moved to the show window and ducked his head so he could see beneath some bridles hanging from the rafters, watching Cooper heading towards the saloon called Waterhole Number One.

Tennison was back. He stiffened when Cooper entered the saloon and strode up to the bar.

'Usual, Coop?' he asked in friendly manner.

'No, Tenn, just gimme a few bottles of that bonded bourbon you freighted in from St Louis.'

Tennison frowned. 'You know I don't sell that stuff over the bar, Coop.'

'Didn't say I was buying – I said *give* 'em to me.'

'What? Like hell! What're you playin' at. . . ?'

Tennison – and every other man in the bar – jumped as the new rifle in Cooper's hands roared. The bullet shattered the big mirror behind the bar and a few bottles and glasses. The barkeeps and Tennison ducked as glass flew.

'New gun,' Cooper said conversationally, levering in a fresh shell. 'Bit touchy on the trigger. Dunno how many times it's likely to do that. So, sooner we get this deal fixed the better, Tenn.'

Tennison's nostrils were pinched and his eyes were slitted. 'All right. I savvy what you're doin'. I ran out so I have to pay, right? Five bottles do you?'

'Sure. And free drinks for whoever wants 'em for the next week.' He waved the rifle barrel casually, freezing Tennison's protest as the drinkers cheered. 'Might be I'll come back and check up – see you're sticking to your part of the deal, Tenno. Be cheaper than building a new saloon.'

'A new. . . ? The hell's that mean?'

'Well, if it should burn down – or something.'

'Christ! And to think I was on your side!'

'But all you did about it was run outta town and hide on your ranch, Tenno. Your convictions weren't strong enough. Now, wrap them bottles well and put 'em in a gunnysack and I'll be on my way – before this here gun goes off again.'

Out in the street, carrying the gunnysack bulging with the bottles of whiskey in one hand, the new Winchester in the other, Cooper slowed his pace as he made towards the livery. The well-dressed man who had been in O'Reardon's store earlier was coming towards him, lifting a hand in greeting.

They met by the stone horse-trough under the shade of the only tree on Main, a gnarled old cotton-wood. A few drops of rain slapped against the dusty leaves.

'Sheriff Cooper. . . ?'

'Not sheriff any longer. Just Chad Cooper.'

The man smiled and thrust out his right hand. 'Tom Christmas . . .' His smile broadened at the somewhat startled look on Cooper's face. He patted his ample belly which didn't look exactly soft but it was straining against his grey vest and polished leather belt. 'I'm used to all the Santa Claus jokes, but it really is my name.'

Cooper transferred the gunnysack and rifle to his left hand and gripped briefly, feeling strength in the man's hand. 'What can I do for you, Mr Christmas?'

'Tom, please . . .' Christmas glanced around as people strolled by, going about their business, a few throwing curious looks at the pair beneath the cotton-wood. He lowered his voice a little – was quite deep and tended to carry. 'I was in that bar last night and witnessed the . . . trouble you had. I was impressed.'

Cooper said nothing, waiting, his face impassive.

Christmas took a deep breath. 'At the time I thought you were the kind of man I could use for a certain . . . chore I have to do. Then in O'Reardon's store I heard you say you hire out your gun for cash . . .' He paused but still Cooper said nothing.

Tom Christmas moved his feet uncomfortably, ran a tongue around his lips.

'Well, what it comes down to, is – I'd like to hire you.'

'For what?'

'To act as my . . . bodyguard.'

Cooper frowned, covering his surprise, but before he could say anything, the other added apologetically,

'Unfortunately, I won't be able to pay you very much. Would two hundred dollars be satisfactory? One hundred when we leave town and the rest when we get back safely. . . ? Or I can post the money with a lawyer in town before we leave if you like. . . .'

'Two hundred? Man, I've just lost five thousand dollars!'

'Yes, I heard. But this will be just a one-off job. There won't be anything for you to do really, except to keep me company.' He gave a quick on-off smile. 'And if things don't turn out the way I expect and . . . something does happen to me . . .' He spread his hands and shrugged. 'Well, you're free to just ride out into the sunset. No strings attached. What d'you say?'

4
Judas Pass

The meeting was to be at sundown in Judas Pass, the high pass through the Coffeepots that was named because an old Apache, long trusted by whites, decided he should not have forsaken his people for so many years and led a wagon-train into a massacre.

The location didn't bother Cooper so much as the time of the meeting.

Sundown could be beautiful in the Coffeepots with the changing colours that seemed to sweep across the varied stone of the canyons and cliffs as if by some giant brush. It could also be a treacherous time, a place filled with shadows that changed position randomly as clouds briefly covered the sun or part of the crimson disc. In Cooper's estimation, it was an ideal place for an ambush.

Tom Christmas laughed out loud when he suggested it. 'Ambush? Hardly! Not for the simple delivery of a harmless package.'

That was all that Cooper knew about the deal: Christmas was to deliver a package to a man who would meet him in the Pass at the appointed time. He was to come alone, exchange the package for another, and then return to Coldwater.

'Doesn't sound like you need a bodyguard at all,' Coop had opined before he had actually agreed to do the job. Christmas had shrugged, smiling – but Cooper noticed that there was a slight tightness at the edge of the smile that prevented it from spreading all the way.

He watched the man's hand fiddle with his belt-buckle and he suddenly knew that despite Tom Christmas's casual approach to the chore, the man was really nervous. And he wasn't making much of a job of hiding it.

'You sure that's all that's involved, Tom?'

The man forced a laugh, lifted his left hand across his chest and pressed it against his heart. 'On my honour! It's just that I don't know this country and I've heard a lot of – unsettling talk about Judas Pass, how outlaws sometimes frequent it or the odd maverick buck will slip away from the reservation just to slit a white throat. Sort of keeping his hand in, as it were – if you'll pardon the pun!'

Cooper frowned: Christmas puzzled him, the way he spoke. Not like a Westerner, that was for sure. Then again, not like a college professor, either, but somewhere in between. And he was occasionally given to a colourful expression that Cooper might have thought nothing of if he had read it in a newspaper or a book, but, spoken in everyday conversation – well, it had him intrigued.

'They say that wagon-train was stopped dead in its tracks by a veritable storm of arrows falling out of the sky, even briefly blotting out the sun. . . .'

That was the kind of thing he would come out with at the most unexpected times.

Cooper tried to probe, find out where Christmas was from, but all he would say was that he moved around a good deal in his job. But he avoided saying what his 'job' was.

Cooper was going to refuse the chore. A payment of $200 was a mere pittance, but then he remembered all he had coming was a month's wages – no big bonus. All he had besides was about $140 he had made fossicking for gold on the ore dumps at an abandoned mine in the Coffeepots.

Two hundred might just help see him through the winter. . . .

So he agreed to accompany Christmas to Judas Pass and now here they were, half-blinded by the sinking sun, another aspect of it that put Cooper on his guard. Tom had said he had been given specific instructions how to approach the Pass, which trail to follow, where to stop by a rock that, by stretching the imagination some, looked like a crouching cougar.

Cooper moved into the rock's shadow. It wasn't very high, in fact about level with his head while he sat his palomino, but at least he could block out some of the glare. He lifted a hand to adjust his hatbrim, watching Christmas from the corner of his eye as the man ran a tongue around his lips, slid his right hand inside his jacket, feeling for something –

likely the package – reassuring himself it was safe.

'Damn you, Christmas! You were told to come alone!'

Cooper's hand dropped to his gun-butt as the voice shouted out of the shadows up ahead. He squinted but could see nothing and cursed the fast-sinking sun. Christmas ran a tongue around his lips and gave a tentative smile as be reached out and placed a hand on Cooper's wrist.

'It's all right,' he said. 'That's the man I'm supposed to meet. I recognize his voice.'

Earlier you said you didn't know who you were going to meet, thought Cooper but he only grunted and eased his grip on the gun-butt while Christmas raised his voice.

'It's all right! He's only a – a guide! I don't know this country and I'd heard some wild tales about Judas Pass. He just brought me along. He'll stay put.'

'He better. Or he's a dead man!' said the voice and Cooper stiffened.

Dead? Sounded a mite more serious than Tom Christmas had led him to believe, but. . . .

'You come ahead and deliver the package, Christmas. Tell your pard he better not try anything.'

'He won't!' Christmas called, gave Cooper a quick shake of the head and heeled his paint forward. 'How far do I come?'

'To the corner of the big rock and then turn right; slow – very slow.'

Cooper watched, intent on Christmas as the man obeyed orders, reached – the corner of the large boulder and turned right – which took him out of sight.

At the same time, Cooper heard a small scratching sound to his left and snapped his head around, right hand starting to lift his gun. He was too late.

A man was crouched on the rock level with his head, and even as he saw him, Cooper jarred as a rifle-butt crashed against his temple, knocking off his hat. He fell from his horse and the man slid down the rock, ran to kneel beside him. Cooper wasn't all the way out but his head roared and hummed and his jaw ached clear down into his shoulder. He felt the trickle of warm blood as it snaked down his face and his hands pressed against the earth as his horse danced away. He was too weak to thrust upright, tried, but fell down again with another grunt. Then his attacker heaved him on to his back and looked down into his face. The man, just a dark silhouette, reared back and swore.

'Judas priest – it's Cooper! Sheriff of Coldwater!'

Not any more, Coop thought, even the words in his mind sounding slurred to him. But he wasn't capable of speaking and concentrated on hearing.

The man beside him raised his voice, 'It's Cooper, Book! Christmas is pullin' somethin' here.'

'Well, he was warned,' answered that voice from the big boulder and the words were swiftly followed by the crash of a sixgun, the shot bounding and echoing through the pass.

'Jesus!' breathed the man beside Cooper as two more men came running up. Cooper thought they carried guns but couldn't be sure. He figured he wasn't going to be able to hang on much longer. . . .

He tried but felt the blackness welling up inside him. He drifted into limbo, the darkness shot through with many colours, and he seemed to fall, grasped wildly at nothing. The roaring in his head grew louder. He felt nauseous, and suddenly there were men talking, but not loudly or clearly enough for him to make out the words.

Then the first boot drove into his side and his big body skidded two feet across the gravel. A big dark shape knelt beside him, fingers twisted in his hair, jerking his head up.

'Where is it?' the shape snarled.

'Wh – where's – what?' Cooper slurred and his head was smashed back against the ground several times. He floated away into near oblivion, feeling hands searching him.

'Check his saddle-bags!' someone snapped.

'Only grub and the usual gear there, Book,' a man answered. 'I already looked.'

Then the big shape swore and hard knuckles cracked back and forth across Cooper's blood-streaked face. Water dashed into his eyes and he gasped, blinking as he was shaken like a rat in a dog's jaws.

'Tell me, you son of a bitch! Tell me where he hid it!'

Cooper made several tries to speak but the words tangled and didn't come out intelligibly. It earned him several more blows and kicks. More water dashed into his face.

'I – I was hired as – bodyguard,' he managed to gasp through his swollen lips.

The big shape snorted. 'Some bodyguard!' He leaned closer and Cooper smelled cloves on his breath. 'Listen, you. I've spent the afternoon at the goddamn dentist and I'm hurtin' and I'm just in the mood to kick your head to mush! I'll only ask you one more time . . .' He pulled out a sixgun, placed the muzzle against Cooper's forehead and cocked the hammer. 'You tell me what I want to know or you're dead. You ain't no use to me if you're gonna stall all the time. . . .'

Cooper coughed and the gun moved away. He spat some blood, tasting its saltiness. He tried to turn over but slid in the loose gravel and realized they had moved him from the original position and he was on a fairly steep slope now. It was too dark to see where it led.

'Stay still!'

'Just – unkinking – my ribs . . . OK. I'll tell you what I know. . . .'

'It better be what I want to hear or. . .' The gun appeared before Cooper's eyes again and the barrel jerked ominously.

'All *right*! I savvy you mean it!' grated Cooper. 'I lost my job as sheriff in Coldwater and this Christmas feller came to me and . . .'

Suddenly, Cooper was a human whirlwind.

Propped on one elbow, he rolled towards the crouching dark shape with the gun and brought up his free hand, flinging a handful of gravel into the startled man's face. There was a yell and the gun went off and Cooper was kicking out wildly. His boot connected with the big man's jaw and he roared and fell on his back, holding his jaw, moaning and spitting: maybe Cooper had loosened his sore tooth. But Cooper didn't stop there. The others moved in and he kicked one man in the knee, bringing him down, cursing and floundering. One of the others crashed into him and fell sprawling. The fourth man held back, calling,

'What the hell? Book. . . ?'

Then Cooper was gone, throwing himself headlong down the dark slope, sliding and rolling as the gravel moved beneath his sore body. He spun so that he slid down feet first, using his hands and elbows as brakes as the slope steepened. He snatched at small rocks to slow his slide. Guns hammered above and he heard the slugs thudding into the slope, one ripping a large chunk of bark off a scraggly tree, ricocheting into the night.

He rolled on to his belly as he grabbed a head-sized boulder, his momentum slowed and he swung his legs in behind the rock and the rest of the clump. He let go and rolled behind them as bullets whined and kicked rockdust over his shoulder. He scrabbled on all fours across the face of the slope, hearing the others cussing as they slid and spilled down the slope. One man rolled past only a few feet away, completely out of control, yelling. Cooper didn't stay to locate the others, he flung himself into the larger rocks, clambered amongst them and over them, dropping down into a tight crevice between two large, bulging boulders. There was room underneath for him to lie flat, panting, ears straining.

He heard boots slipping on the rocks above, men's

breath rasping, twice smelled their sweat they were so close.

'Where's the son of a bitch gone!' someone gasped.

'I know where he'll be goin' when I find him!' growled another and Cooper recognized the voice of the big man who had beaten him and originally called out to Tom Christmas. 'Two of you mount up and search the Pass! It'll be quicker. Morg, you and me'll search these rocks.'

'I don't think he knows anythin', Book.'

Book made a snorting sound. 'He knows what happened here, don't he? He's a witness. You see him, you shoot to kill!'

Cooper crouched, swearing when he found he had somehow lost his sixgun during the slide. His rifle was in the saddle scabbard on the palomino but that wasn't going to do him any good. He felt around, found an apple-sized rock that fitted his hand well. He hefted it. Yeah – he could crack a man's skull easily with this. Trouble was, if they got that close to him they'd shoot him before he could even raise his arm.

Somehow they must have missed the crevice between the rocks. He heard them time and again crunching over the rock above. Some grit even drifted down on his head, dislodged by the killers' boots. But no one found the crevice or looked down. They would have a hard job finding him in this pitch black, anyway, but . . .

He stiffened when he heard the clatter of hoofs.

'See him?'

'Nary a sign, Book – I reckon he's give us the slip or fallen amongst them rocks and broke his neck.'

'I could wish for that. But I'd rather know for sure . . .'

'Hell, he don't know nothin'. I reckon he's just set on savin' his own neck now. Christmas couldn't've paid him much.'

'No, you're right there,' mused Book. Cooper held his breath, the man sounded so close. He must be standing almost directly above him. 'Right! We'd be better lookin' for that package Christmas has hid on us . . .'

'Too bad you shot him so quick, Book.'

Book's voice told Cooper he didn't like anyone pointing out that obvious fact.

'Mebbe I'll do a bit more shootin' before this night is over! Soon as you said the sheriff was with him I figured it had to be a trap and I didn't aim to let Christmas go no matter what. He'd give me a package that I thought was what we wanted. Was only after I'd shot him that I opened it and found it was nothing but some squares of cardboard.'

'Well, what we gonna do?' The man who spoke sounded nervous. 'I don't like standin' around like this when that Coop's still on the loose. He's one tough *hombre* . . .'

'All right. We'd best clear the Pass. Head back for the hideout tonight and we'll figure out how to track down Christmas's package tomorrow.'

After they had gone, Cooper stayed hidden for twenty minutes – and just as well he did. Something in Book's voice had warned him the man wasn't really aiming to give up so easily. He was about to climb out of his hiding place when he froze at the sound of Book's voice.

'Looks like the sonuver's really gone. Let's hightail it this time. The night stage to Socorro'll be due through the Pass pretty soon.'

Cooper listened, heard the horses' sounds dwindling away through the dark. He waited a further twenty minutes, then climbed out warily, crouched, and looked around. His vision wasn't the best and he felt sluggish and disoriented, but he could make out the slide marks on the slope in the faint light of the quarter moon. He clambered back up and found where they had beaten him. It was just behind Cougar Rock and he located his fallen sixgun before seeing the palomino cropping a patch of grass. The saddle had been removed and the stitching cut. *So the package can't be all that big*, he thought as he looked at his ravaged saddle-bags. His rifle was there luckily and he led the horse back into the Pass and around the big rock where he had last seen Tom Christmas.

He found him almost right away. The man had been shot in the back of the head, his hair scorched by the gun flash, his skull split wide open.

His clothes had been torn from him and ripped apart. His saddle and bags, too, had been cut up. He hunkered down beside Christmas, put a hand out to touch the dead man's shoulder lightly.

Yeah, Book, whoever you are – you were right about one thing . . .

I was sure one hell of a bodyguard!

5
Conscience

A small crowd gathered and followed Cooper's progress down Main as he rode in on his dusty palomino, leading the paint with its blanket-draped body roped over the saddle. They flung questions at him but he didn't answer, climbed down at the hitch rail outside Doctor Peebles' house and carried the body inside.

The doctor didn't need to examine it to see the cause of death and told Cooper so, looking at him strangely.

'Who is it?' He began to treat Cooper's injuries.

'Feller gave his name as Tom Christmas. Had some kind of package to deliver to someone in Judas Pass at sundown. Hired me as bodyguard.'

Peebles held Cooper's steady gaze a moment and then nodded. 'I take it things went badly wrong.' He painted iodine on one of Cooper's cuts and rubbed arnica into the bruises.

'They did, Doc. Mostly my fault. I took him at his word that there was really nothing to it – hell, he was only paying a couple of hundred. But it didn't set right and – well, I never took things seriously enough and now.' He gestured to the body spread out on the doctor's operating table and buttoned up his shirt again. 'Thanks, Doc.'

The medic continued to gaze at Cooper, then said quietly, 'Tell me what happened.'

Cooper was kind of surprised at the relief he felt after he had given a brief description of events. Peebles pursed his lips.

'Can hardly blame yourself, Chad. It was obviously a set-up and I'd say they intended to kill Christmas all along, as soon as they had this mysterious package. No clue as to what it was?'

Cooper shook his head, brought out a torn and dirt-smeared brown-paper wrapper and three mangled pieces of cardboard that had been cut from a soap carton. They were about twice the size of a playing card.

'This fooled the one called Book for a moment before he killed Christmas. I guess it was some kind of small notebook Tom was supposed to hand over.'

'Could be. But I suppose there could be several things about that size and weight . . . folded documents, a tintype picture or postcard, an engraving plate – though this Book would've felt the weight and realized it wasn't what he was expecting.' Peebles pulled a sheet over the dead man. 'I take it you won't be leaving town just yet.'

Cooper gave him a quick look, shook his head.

'Like I said, Doc, I wasn't much of a bodyguard. I took a hundred bucks from Tom Christmas. I didn't earn it. I figure to try to give him some value for his money, even though it won't do him much good now.'

'But it'll do you some good.'

Cooper smiled faintly. 'Sharp old sonuver, ain't you, Doc?' He sighed. 'Yeah, well I should've taken better precautions. Was still kind of mad about this town pulling back on my bonus and I wasn't caring as much as I should've.'

Peebles smiled. 'The day you arrived, I picked you as a man of conscience, Chad. I'm sorry about what happened with that bonus but . . .' he paused, 'you realize the town's just waiting for you to leave now?'

'What's it matter to them? I'm no longer sheriff. It's not costing them a red cent for me to stay on.'

'No-oo. But there's been talk. That McPherson came in with his gunslingers to kill you. They're afraid other men with grudges against you might also come to town.'

Cooper snorted. 'They do and I'll kill 'em. But I'll be hanging around for a while, Doc. Leastways, till I find out where Tom Christmas came from and what was behind his murder. You never noticed him around town?'

'Can't say I did. I guess you'll be checking the hotels and so on? He had to stay somewhere. . . .'

Cooper nodded. 'I know he was here last night because he was in the Drovers' when I nailed McPherson. I'll be moving along, Doc. You arrange his burial? I'll pay for it.'

Peebles smiled and shook his head slowly as he showed Cooper out. 'Like I said – a man of conscience.'

Cooper's enquiries produced little and he found many folk hostile towards him. They wanted him to quit town, all right, leave Coldwater in peace in case his presence – without a badge to back him now – brought in the old enemies who would try to square away their grudges on the streets of the town.

Feeney told him that Christmas had stalled his paint in his livery mid-afternoon yesterday.

'Told me he wasn't sure when he'd be needin' it but to grain an' groom him and have him more or less ready to go at a moment's notice.' Feeney was surly but seemed co-operative enough. Which puzzled Cooper a little, because the man was a grudge-holder, unforgiving. He couldn't tell Coop which hotel Christmas went to after leaving the livery.

None of the hotels had rented Christmas a room so Cooper tried the boarding-house. At the third one he learned that the man had booked a room – just overnight.

'Said he would be leaving town the next day,' the woman who ran the place told him.

To meet Book and his pards in Judas Pass, thought Cooper. He asked to see the man's room, but the woman said it had already been let to someone else.

'He didn't leave any gear here? Warbag? Bedroll, anything like that?'

She shook her head. 'He brought his saddle-bags

with him and took them when he left,' she told him. 'That was all.'

Cooper left. He knew this wasn't going to be as straightforward as he had figured.

But by all counts, Christmas had been in town for more than twelve hours before he had approached Cooper about the bodyguard job. Somebody had to have seen him. . . .

'Feeney!' he said aloud and some women passing by started and gave him a strange look as he strode across the street towards the livery's open doors.

Feeney was in the office. When he saw Cooper's purposeful stride he started for the rear door. But Cooper lunged in and reached out and slammed it even as the livery man started out, so fast that his face smacked into the wood. He yelled and clapped a hand to his nose and mouth. He spun, shoulders against the door now, eyes widening as Cooper leaned a long arm against the planks, across Feeney's shoulder, effectively pinning him in place.

'Too much chili again, Feen?'

The man swallowed, said nothing, examined his hand, but there was no blood although his nose and mouth would be bruised.

'What'd you do with Christmas's gear? Sold it yet? Or aimed to, I'll bet?'

'Dunno what you're talkin' about! Gear? He only left his hoss with me.'

'How anyone ever elected you to the town council beats me.' Cooper leaned closer. 'Feeney, you're a goddamn liar. Tom stayed at the Clover Leaf rooming-house and Mrs Lipson said he only came – and went – with his saddle-bags. He didn't have a warbag or bedroll when we rode up into Judas Pass so he must've left 'em with you.'

Feeney shook his head. 'I never seen 'em – I swear Coop!'

'Can't take your word for it, Feen.' Cooper grabbed the man by the throat and flung him across the office. Feeney skidded into his desk, papers flying like a snowstorm. Cooper strode towards him and the man flung his arms across his face. 'Just get 'em, Feen, and save yourself a lot of pain.'

Feeney apparently figured this made good sense and fetched a travel-stained warbag from behind a grain-bin just outside the office. 'I ain't touched anythin' . . .'

'But you were going to,' Cooper said flatly and Feeney didn't deny it, just stood with a hangdog expression while Cooper opened the bedroll and warbag. 'Go about your business, Feeney. But stay where you can hear me holler if I want you.'

Feeney hurried out, rubbing his throat, bruised mouth working – but silently.

There was nothing in the bedroll although Cooper only gave it a cursory search, having a hunch that if he was going to find anything at all it would be in the warbag. There was a letter addressed to *Mr & Mrs Thomas Christmas, 11 Blackwood St., Santa Fe, NM.* The date was three months ago and it was telling 'Tom and Lu' that the writer was sorry but he couldn't make it for a visit because of an 'assignment' that would take him to Alaska. It was signed *Pete Gilbert* and there was a PS: *You know who to see about this. As for 'B' – bad cess to the s.o.b!*

Cooper folded it slowly and put it in his shirt pocket. Seemed to him like part of the letter was missing. Why would anyone have to 'see' someone because Gilbert couldn't pay a visit? Then he pounced on a black notebook he found tucked into the bottom of a woollen sock. It was small and leather-bound – and totally unintelligible. It was a mass of squiggles and curls and angular lines, like no writing Cooper had ever seen before. The only other thing of interest amongst Christmas's gear was a book called *Ivanhoe* by Sir Walter Scott. He flicked through, mildly interested to find that the story was about knights of old: even the famous English outlaw Robin Hood seemed to be featured. There was a slip of paper Christmas had used as a bookmark – this was where a quick scan showed him Robin Hood was a character in the story – but there didn't seem to be any other inserts. He held the heavy, leather-bound, embossed covers by the edges and shook the book upside down. Nothing fell out.

But he felt a slight bulge in the rear cover and when he pressed his thumb around its outline, it seemed to be a square of something about three inches around.

He slit the bookbinder's stitching and took out an envelope with a square of something in it. When he unwrapped it, he found it was glass, smoky with grey and black shapes when he held it up to the light.

A photographic plate. And there was a name scratched into the glass border.

Painted Desert Studios.

Chad Cooper smiled. Hell, it was just down the street, about half-way along the block!

Rosanna Cisco was regarded as just a bit 'odd' by the townsfolk of Coldwater. Not only because she was a woman and ran her own business – there weren't many of those around in the West unless running some sort of feminine frippery shop or the madam of a brothel – but because of the nature of her business.

She was a woman ahead of her time – a lady photographer. Not only that, she sold her work as far away as New York and San Francisco and did regular business with such publications as *Harper's Weekly*. Still, she was well regarded in the town because she gave generously to charity and helped the poor: she didn't just give money, she went and physically helped, washing and ironing clothes, house-cleaning, and she would find work for the husbands, too. If they were the lazy type, they were soon straightened out by Rosanna or else she publicly shamed them.

She was a person who got things done.

Chad Cooper had met her several times during his stay in Coldwater and had gotten along well with her. But, being an outspoken type, she had told him that while she understood the need for violence in his job as sheriff, she thought he was too ready and willing to use it as a means of settling problems.

'In this job, Rosa, you're either fast or last, and I'm still walking around so I reckon my way works.'

She had taken his blunt reply well enough and hadn't mentioned her views since.

Now she looked at the photographic plate as they stood in the working part of her studio which was hung with various painted canvas backdrops for use in studio photography.

She was a tallish woman, dark haired and dark eyed, skin a touch dusky because of Spanish fore-bears way back in her ancestry. 'Yes, this is mine – I didn't realize it was missing.'

'You want to check and make sure?'

'I am sure,' she told him but saw that lawman's look in his eyes and smiled faintly. 'All right – I'll check.'

It took but a couple of minutes as she looked into a deep file-drawer with many thick padded folders of plates similar to the one Cooper had brought in. All were neatly catalogued in separate pockets. One was empty and she tapped the plate she held.

'This is it – he must've taken it while I was out of the room.'

'He being Tom Christmas?'

'Yes. In answer to your next question, you may remember I earned myself a little publicity by taking a panorama shot of our Fourth of July celebration parade?'

Cooper recalled it. Something she had devised herself, a long series of individual photos, slightly overlapping, so that when she developed them and printed them in one long strip, matching the overlaps precisely, it showed the big parade filling the entire length of Main Street, *Harper's* ran it in a special mid-section and it was picked up by East Coast magazines and papers as well. Not that panorama pictures hadn't been done before, but Rosa had taken her shots over a period of hours and by judicious developing of the plates had managed to produce an overall soft-lighting effect that was so similar over the nine plates used in the strip that it appeared as if the photograph had been taken in a single shot. She had earned high praise, though some folk claimed she must have had expert help. She put that down as just another swipe at her femininity.

'Christmas asked if it was possible for him to have an enlargement of *part* of the strip,' the woman told Cooper. 'I said it might be difficult but he waved that part aside – all he wanted was this section.' She tapped the plate that Cooper had brought. 'It's part of plate number five, midway along the street. Although he said he only wanted a small group of his friends I sensed that he was chiefly interested in just this man and woman. I projected the number five plate on to the wall, in negative, of course, and he showed me which part he wanted enlarged. Not only did he want the two people in it, he also wanted the background with O'Reardon's General Store in the picture, and a portion of the street parade which had one of the leading banners, with the name Coldwater, Arizona, on it, plus the date of the parade – July Fourth, 1886.'

She paused and looked at Cooper thoughtfully, as if considering her next words.

'It wasn't an easy thing to arrange and keep in good enough focus so the signs could be read, but I like a challenge and told him I'd try – but it would cost more than a normal enlargement.'

'That faze him any?'

'I – think my price startled him a little but only for a moment. He told me to go ahead and wanted to know if he could pick it up in an hour.' She smiled. 'I told him to come back in two days – and that seemed to bother him but he accepted it and even said he should've expected that but he had been so long away from such things that . . .' She shrugged. 'He never finished the sentence.'

Cooper leaned closer. 'You know what he meant?'

'I think he was saying that he knew something about the photographic business – which I had suspected from the way he told me exactly what he wanted so confidently – but he stopped because it was something that just slipped out.'

'Something he hadn't meant to say.'

'Yes.'

'You think he was another photographer?'

'No. But he knew a bit about it. Not much, really.'

'How would he pick up whatever he knew?'

'Oh, maybe he worked on a newspaper at some time.'

That struck home with Cooper and he held up his hand quickly. 'That's it! He had a funny way of talking. No, not funny – but he was better-spoken than most Westerners and yet he didn't seem like a college man . . .'

'Probably a journalist – that was my impression of him.' She seemed a little fussed now.

Cooper couldn't help but smile. 'I'm glad I came to see you, Rosa.' He dug out the letter he had taken off Christmas and showed it to her while he held the small notebook with the strange writing. She took it slowly, almost reluctantly. She glanced at the letter.

'Peter S. Gilbert was a well-known freelance journalist, always went to adventurous or dangerous locations for his stories. I – knew him slightly.' She sounded a little breathless. 'He died in Alaska, couple of months ago, killed when ice crushed his canoe on some half-frozen river.'

Cooper nodded, handing her the notebook. 'Then I reckon this could be a journalist's notes written in the shorthand they use . . .'

'Yes – it looks like it.' Rosa flicked through the pages then stopped suddenly. 'This isn't standard Pitman's, though. A lot of journalists develop their own private style to protect their notes on special stories. It ensures rivals don't steal their thunder.' She sounded shaky but her words knocked the edge of Cooper's first surge of elation.

'Are you saying that's what's in that notebook?'

'Afraid so, Chad – I couldn't read this in a fit. It might just as well be written in Egyptian hieroglyphics.'

6
Target

It wasn't entirely a wasted visit. Although Rosa Cisco
said she could not read the notebook found in Tom
Christmas's warbag – they couldn't even be certain it
belonged to Tom – she said there were a few words
she recognized as standard journalistic shorthand so
it could well be a mix of this and private shorthand.

'Let me spend a little time on it, Chad – I may be
able to work something out.'

He looked uncertain as well as disappointed but
nodded, saying, 'Maybe not too long, Rosa – I might
have to start down another trail if you can't crack that
quickly.'

She looked shrewdly at his face and the marks of
the beating. 'You're in danger?'

He shrugged. 'I'm always in danger.'

'That's true – and I've often wondered why you
persist in your – profession.'

'It's what I do best.'

'Yes, you're certainly good at it – but I suspect you

enjoy the danger. Oh, maybe you don't realize it, but . . .'

'You're too damn smart for a woman.'

She laughed. 'Oh, I could tear that remark to shreds, but I see you're impatient now to get on with your investigation. Would you like a look at this plate projected on a screen? You won't be able to make out people's features very well, but I can show you the part Tom Christmas was interested in – and make you an enlargement if you want.'

'Sure.' He took the pieces of cut cardboard from his pocket and showed her. 'Tom handed these over, it seems, and they were good enough to fool this *hombre* called Book for a minute or two.'

'Well, that's about the size of enlargement he wanted. Postcard size. "Easily carried in a pocket" he said.'

'OK – I'll call back later.'

'Not before tonight.'

He waved and left, wondering where Tom Christmas had been for the two days it took Rosa to make the enlargement for him.

He made for O'Reardon's and the storekeeper wasn't pleased to see him.

'Your packages are waitin' out the back.'

'Fine. Pick 'em up later. That feller that was in here last time . . .'

'The one you got killed, you mean?' the storekeeper said with a sneer of vindictiveness.

Cooper's cold eyes held him and O'Reardon dropped his gaze quickly. 'Yeah, that one. He come in here before?'

'No.'

'Anyone speak with him before I came in?'

O'Reardon hesitated, then nodded. 'Big feller. Long hair down to his shoulders. Smelled like cloves.'

Cooper tensed. 'Christmas call him anything? Book, maybe?'

'Dunno – the big feller did all the talkin'. He poked Christmas in the chest with his finger and it must've been hard because Christmas staggered, had to grab the edge of the counter to keep from fallin'. He said somethin' like, "Just get it! An' deliver it like you're s'posed to. We'll deal, but only on our terms . . ." '

'That last part seem to worry Christmas?'

'*All* of it worried him! He dithered around and I spoke to him several times but he never heard me. Was thinkin' of somethin' else, I guess. Then you showed up.'

'OK, Pat – you've done good.' Cooper slapped some money down on the counter. 'That'll cover most of the stores you packed for me. I'll be back later for 'em.'

The storekeeper couldn't believe his luck but he snatched up the money, counted it, and as Cooper left, called, 'They'll be ready whenever you want 'em, Chad.'

Cooper went to one of the town's back streets where he found Coldwater's lone dentist. The place smelled heavily of liquor for Doc Francis had a habit of getting his patients drunk before extracting teeth. He claimed he couldn't afford 'them newfangled knock-out gases. Rotgut's cheaper'.

He said he remembered the man Cooper described, but didn't know his name. 'Had an abscess on a molar. Drank nigh on a whole pint of red-eye and still yelled like a Comanche. Fact, I was a mite worried, figured he might tear my head off, but he paid, all right, and I threw in a bottle of oil of cloves 'cause he said he had another tooth that was achin' but he didn't aim for me to touch it.'

'Anyone with him?'

'Two hardcase types. One of 'em was tryin' hard not to laugh and the feller with the long hair threw him down the stairs when they were leavin'.'

At least he knew Book and his pards had been in town at the same time as Christmas and they must have set up the ambush in Judas Pass. Tom's hiring Cooper as a bodyguard had thrown them a little but they had still killed him.

Cooper prowled the town, questioning Feeney again, checking the saloons. He even went to see Cy Maloney but the man feigned sleep and refused to speak with him.

Then, after a meagre supper in one of the town's diners, Cooper made his way towards Rosa Cisco's studio. He was walking across the mouth of Candle Lane, just past the druggist's, when a gun blasted and his hat was wrenched from his head.

Cooper hit the dirt rolling and when he flopped on to his belly, his sixgun was in his hand and working, blasting three fast shots into the darkness of the lane.

He heard a clatter of falling crates and empty bottles, then running boots. He leapt up and charged in – realizing too late he had made a mistake.

His big frame was silhouetted against the lights on Main and a gun crashed from the alley. *There were two of them!* he thought as the bullet seared his side and spun him hard against the clapboard wall of the druggist's. Another bullet ripped splinters from the same wall and stung his face. He dropped to one knee as a third shot sent a slug over his head. Somewhere across Main he heard glass shatter.

Then he was stretched out, hugging the wall base, Colt thrust out in front of him. Someone was running and this time he knew they were quitting the lane for the safety of the darkness in the vacant, weed-grown lot beyond. He triggered, rose to one knee and reloaded before heaving to his feet.

He pressed a hand against his bleeding side and went warily, but as swiftly as he could, into the darkness. He heard the weeds being crushed by the escaping ambushers, glimpsed the vague, dark shapes crossing the lot, dodging the trash that had been dumped amongst the weeds. Panting a little, he leaned against a crooked fence behind the rooming-house at the end of the lane, lifted his gun in both hands and drew bead on the closer of the two running men. They were both crouched over, and one might have seen him because a gun fired although he didn't hear where the bullet went.

He led his man who was zigzagging wildly, missed with his first shot, eased his shoulder against the fence for a more comfortable position and triggered again. The man went down soundlessly, thrashing

briefly, hidden by the long weeds. The first man hesitated, then ran on. Cooper stepped out and fired
again, but missed.

He ran to where the first man had gone down but
he was still and there was no pulse in his neck.
Cooper rammed the man's sixgun into his belt and
gave chase.

His side was bleeding copiously now, wetting his
shirt and the waistband of his trousers. Pain was starting but he gritted his teeth and ran on. The man
ahead must have panicked when he saw that Cooper
was persevering, because he emptied his pistol in a
wild volley, stumbled and then cleared the low wire
fence at the far side of the lot.

Cooper cut across, stumbled himself, but ran
down the edge of the weeds and wasn't far behind
the killer when he reached the fence. He slowed a
little, eased himself over, and then heard the man
running along the creekbank. Cooper stayed close to
the fence, for the ground was firmer here, and when
he heard the man splash into the creek, intending to
cross it, he thrust through the brush, came out on
the bank and saw his quarry waist-deep.

'Hold it! Your gun's empty and you make a mighty
fine target against the water!'

The man snapped his head around, but continued
across, tearing at the water with his hands, one holding his empty Colt. Cooper waited until the man was
starting to climb up the steep, lighter-coloured bank,
then he put a bullet into him. The man grunted and
was punched into the muddy bank by the impact.
Then he slid slowly back into the water, face down.

Cooper swore: he looked like he was dead.

Cooper waded across, the water stinging his wound, turned the man over on to his back, and heaved him half-way up the bank. He sat down, breathing hard, pressing a hand into his side in an attempt to stop the bleeding. A few men came running up to see what was wrong, and Cooper said to the nearest,

'Strike a match and hold it close to his face.'

The man did so and in the flare, Cooper looked at the face of the killer. It was mud-streaked, running with water. It wasn't anyone he knew by name but he thought he had seen him hanging around the saloons for a couple of days. Likely some hardcase who had tried to turn a dollar with his gun. . . .

'D'you think he was a man sent in by Tom Christmas's killers?' asked Doc Peebles as he tied off the last suture in Cooper's wound.

Chad grimaced and shook his head. 'I dunno, Doc. Maybe. The other feller was a down-and-out. Neither were pros – but they sure used pros up at Judas Pass.'

'Why would they jump you and try to kill you? They sound like the type who would drag you into the lane, beat you senseless, then go through your pockets.'

Cooper looked up sharply. 'Yeah. Something to think about, Doc. . . .'

When he left he resumed his way to Rosa Cisco's studio but this time stayed in lighted areas, carrying his rifle, a bullet in the chamber, thumb on the hammer.

No one tried anything and the woman met him at the door and pulled him inside quickly.

'I heard about what happened . . . I thought you might not come.' She smiled at the look he gave her. 'See, I was right? You do enjoy the danger!'

'I didn't enjoy the bullet across the ribs. How did the enlargement turn out?'

'Come and see for yourself.'

There really wasn't much to see, not on a postcard-size photographic print. She gave him a magnifying glass and he studied the print closely; it showed a section of the crowd watching the parade outside of O'Reardon's store. Rosa pointed with a pencil to a man and a woman.

'Those were the two he was interested in – or perhaps only one of them, but they were together.'

A big man, tall, broad shouldered, well set up and dressed like a gambler in what looked to be grey frockcoat and pinstripe trousers. His facial features were small but clear enough, his main feature being a pointed chin and heavy eyebrows. The woman looked like a whore to Cooper, a whore who had been dressed tastefully under supervision, maybe just for this occasion. There was some sort of mark just above her fairly low-cut neckline but Rosa said it was only a speck on the plate. She looked vaguely familiar to Cooper.

'Well, you can read the signs clearly,' Cooper said. 'No mistaking where or when it was taken. Maybe that's what's so interesting, not the people.'

She shook her head. 'No, he was definite that those two people had to be in the picture. There were several better sections of the panorama that could have shown the location if that was all he had wanted.'

'OK. Can I keep this?'

'Yes – I've made an extra copy if you want that, too.'

'No, you hold that – and the plate, if that's OK?'

'Of course.' She gathered her things and as she put them away in a cupboard, said casually over her shoulder, 'They say you killed both those men tonight.'

'That's what they were trying to do to me. But I only meant to wing the one in the creek. He slipped back and the bullet took him high. I'd've liked to have talked with him.'

She closed the cupboard, turned and leaned back against it. 'I can imagine the way you would "talk" to him!'

He arched his eyebrows. 'I wanted information. I don't have any ambitions to walk these streets just to be a damn. target . . .'

She sighed. 'No, I – I suppose it is your life you're laying on the line.'

'For no pay,' he added flatly, a mite tired of these criticisms. No one worried about his methods when he tamed down this town from a hell-hole to a law-abiding place, but now. . . . He touched a hand to his hatbrim. 'Work out how much I owe you and I'll pay you next time I see you. Thanks for your help.'

She started to speak but saw he was angry – and

she had made him that way. As he stepped out into the night, she said,

'The one in the creek was named Penn, so I was told. He used to do odd jobs around the livery and the Waterhole.'

He paused, nodded without looking back, and stepped out into the night.

He walked warily but they almost got him.

This time it was done professionally, from a rooftop – from behind the high falsefront on the feed-and-grain store, not half a block from his rooming-house.

The bullet fanned his cheek at the same time as he heard the whiplash of the rifle and he dived headlong to the left, using his instinct. The second shot, coming from the roof above Murphy's barbershop, slammed through the space he had occupied a split second before.

They were good, co-ordinating their fire, the first gun hammering lead into the boardwalk he lay beside, knowing his instinctive reaction would be to roll away from it, and the second man was already shooting where he figured his body would be.

They might be pros, but Chad Cooper had been shot at from ambush countless times during his career and his brain was working overtime, figuring their moves *and* his own simultaneously. So instead of thrusting away from the splintered edge of the boardwalk, he rolled beneath it, flattening himself to squeeze under where there was more room.

The bullets raked the ground and kicked stones and grit under the boards, too, and he squinted, hit his head on a beam as he slithered back quickly, got amongst the support poles and flung himself forward. He still had his rifle and he glimpsed a movement against the stars above the falsefront on the grain store, got off two fast shots. He saw wood slivers erupt, then a man screamed, reared up, clawing at his face. His rifle clattered on to the awning below and the man himself stumbled about, past the highest part of the falsefront that he had been using as cover, and jack-knifed over the low section. His body crashed thunderously on to the awning, dust rising around the damaged shingles. Then he rolled into the street, falling heavily, floundering.

'Milt!' he croaked, raising one arm in the general direction of the barbershop.

Cooper saw the movement up there and swung his smoking rifle barrel across but before he could fire, the man up there put two bullets into the one lying in the street, the body shuddering.

The action froze Cooper briefly. *Christ! The man on the roof had risked his own neck just to put two shots into his pard so he couldn't talk!*

These were not only pros – but *ruthless* ones!

By then the killer had turned his rifle on to Cooper's hiding-place, emptied the magazine at him, the bullets smashing into the planks above him, spewing grit into his face, stinging his neck and under his eyes.

Unable to see he triggered blindly, heard his lead punching into clapboards. Then, blinking, clawing at watering eyes, he heard the sound of racing hoofs as the killer hightailed it out of town.

Cooper lunged out into the street, intending to go after the man but realized that by the time he'd saddled up the man would be well away. No doubt he not only had his escape route planned, but, being the professional he was, there could be a third man waiting along the trail. . . .

So Cooper slowed and as folk came warily out of their houses into the street he walked across to the dead man.

He recognized him as one of the men who had jumped him in Judas Pass, sidekick to the mysterious and brutal 'Book'.

Looked like they wanted to finish him off along with poor Tom Christmas.

Well, he would see about that.

7
Coop's Way

Feeney was scared enough to tell the truth.

He pressed back against the warped planks of his stable wall as Cooper faced him, no more than a foot away, not saying anything, just staring at the man with hard eyes.

'Penn did roustabout work for you,' Cooper said finally after Feeney had lifted both hands as a sign of surrender. 'What was the name of his sidekick?'

The livery man's lips were scaled dry with his fear and he licked them several times before answering. 'He – he used to hang around with a feller named McCoy . . .'

'Describe him.'

Feeney did so, haltingly, and Cooper nodded: it fitted the man he had killed in Candle Lane earlier. 'But they never done no work for me for a long time,' Feeney added quickly. 'They did swampin' and roustaboutin' at the Waterhole . . . They got to drink the dregs of the bottles that way.'

It had been a long time since Feeney had told the truth about anything but Cooper believed him this time. He nodded and stepped back and the livery man's jaw sagged as he cringed, expecting a blow as Cooper's right hand lifted. But it only touched him lightly on the shoulder and his knees felt like rubber as Cooper said,

'*Gracias*, Feen . . . But you know I'll be back if your info doesn't check out.'

Feeney knew and sweated a gallon before Cooper had even left the stables.

Tennison didn't want to see Cooper and was actually in the act of saddling his mount so as to ride out to his ranch again, when the big ex-lawman found him behind his saloon in his private, stone-walled stable.

'Doing the chores for yourself now, Tenn? Little earlier and you could've had Penn or McCoy save you the trouble.'

The saloon man spun, dropping the bridle, the big black gelding moving back with a snort. 'What –? Penn? McCoy? Haven't seen 'em around for a spell.'

'You want 'em you'll find 'em out at Boot Hill. And I don't see how come you wouldn't know they got killed trying to bushwhack me earlier, Tenn. Weren't they s'posed to report back to you after they did the job?'

Tennison was about to deny it but he knew Cooper of old and saved his breath. He waited expectantly and grew more nervous the longer the silence dragged on, finally blurting,

'It was Cy! He told me to hire 'em!'

'And you did it.'

The saloon man looked around as if for help, then seemed to slump. 'Well – I was kinda pissed at you, Coop. Cy was, too, still is. If he could move around, he'd try to kill you himself . . .'

Cooper moved in on the saloon man and then Tennison looked past him at the same time as Cooper heard a sound at the entrance to the stables.

He spun and saw two of Tennison's bouncers coming at him, with their leather-bound, nailhead-studded billies. Coop jumped to one side as the first club whistled past him but the second one caught him just below the bullet-burned ribs and he grunted, swayed, fell to one knee.

'Beat him down!' Tennison yelled.

The bouncers tried. They moved in fast, billies raised, boots ready to swing. Cooper, instead of trying to get up, dived headlong for the floor and swung his rifle savagely. It cracked across the shins of the nearest man who howled and danced away awkwardly. He cannoned into the second man, knocking him off balance, but he swore and thrust his hurt companion aside.

Too late. Cooper was on his feet now and the rifle butt came up under the big man's jaw. Bone cracked and teeth splintered and the mouth was bloody and broken as the bouncer fell unconscious. The one with the hurt shins was down on his side and Cooper kicked him in the head, putting him out of the fracas.

Tennison was already running into the night. Cooper stepped out of the stables and triggered a shot into the air.

'Next one's got your name on it, Tenn!'

The man stopped, panting, lifting his hands, turning slowly, face a sickly yellow in the faint lamplight, eyes wide. His jaw was quivering in fear as Cooper approached.

He grabbed the saloon man by his shirtfront and dragged him past the gathering crowd of drinkers, through the bar and out on to Main. He hauled him stumbling, pleading, all the way to Doc Peebles' and then around to the back where the medico had a small insulated shed that acted as a morgue. It was cold and damp inside, the blocks of ice melting slowly. Tennison pulled back as Cooper lowered the ceiling lamp on its chain above the sheet-covered body on the narrow table. It was the man who had been killed by his own pard from the roof of the barber's. Cooper threw back the sheet.

'Take a good look, Tenn. You see him in your bar tonight? While you're thinking about your answer, think about your two bouncers. You're within easy reach of my rifle-barrel.'

It was persuasion enough, Tennison nodded. 'He was in earlier. Name's Eddie someone. Runs with Milt Downey. Both hardcases for hire. Come from across the line in Colorado. I had nothin' to do with 'em tryin' to shoot you, Coop! I swear! Penn an' McCoy, OK, I did what Cy wanted, but this – no, sir!'

'All right, Tenn. But this is gonna cost you another three bottles of that bonded whiskey.'

'Hell almighty, Coop! That stuff costs a fortune to ship in! I – oh, all right. I guess it'll save me some dental work.'

'You're right there. Eddie someone and Milt Downey, right?'

'They come in sometimes when they're passin' through – I don't have much to do with 'em. Eddie's a boozer.'

But Cooper was walking away into the night and Tennison pulled out a kerchief and mopped his dripping face. He needed a mighty good slug of some of that bonded whiskey himself – *and right now!*

Cooper found the old law-office padlocked but he smashed the lock off with the butt of his rifle and went into the musty room. He lit the lamps and sat down in the creaky old swivel-chair at the desk which was still covered with his clutter from when he was wearing a badge. He opened the middle desk-drawer and pulled out a thick pile of Wanted dodgers, began leafing through them.

It took him two hours before he found what he wanted. He had missed it a couple of times, too eagerly looking at the sketched faces of the wanted men and the names underneath. But when he began to read the smaller print, he found aliases listed and beneath the smeared likeness of a man who called himself 'Reid Partridge' he found one of his aliases was 'Eddie Reid', a member of an outlaw gang wanted in Utah and Colorado, led by Jay Booker.

'Booker!' he murmured loud. ' "Book" for short?'

He pawed through the Wanted dodgers again, this time reading the smaller print on each one and found one without any illustration, only a vague description of the man. Amongst his many aliases in faint, smeared print was 'J.G. Booker'. Someone had written in faint pencil in a scrawled hand, 'see back'.

Cooper turned over the dog-eared paper and there was a list of names written in pencil under the heading of 'One-time Gang Members – (some still members).'

Amongst the names were Eddie Reid and Milt Downey.

So now he knew where the pros came from – and it seemed they were out to kill him. But why? Simply because he had been at Judas Pass? It would make more sense if they had tried to capture him and work on him some more to see if he knew where the package was that Tom Christmas had been going to deliver.

Murder seemed a mite drastic, but then these were ruthless sonuvers and one more human life would mean no more to them than stomping on a cockroach. . . .

Then a cold knot suddenly formed in his belly.

The letter he had found amongst Tom's gear had been addressed to Christmas *and Mrs* Christmas at a Santa Fe address.

'Goddamnit!' he said aloud and left the office hurriedly, the lamps still burning, the door open behind him as he ran down the street towards his rooming-house, rifle in hand, folk giving him a wide berth.

What if this 'Book' or someone amongst his pards realized that Tom Christmas had a wife?

They would take a lot of convincing that she wasn't a part of whatever he had been up to . . .

Which would be too bad for Mrs Christmas. . . .

He stopped at the railroad depot and told the sleepy duty man to hold the Denver train when it arrived. 'Hey, Coop! I cain't do that! I ain't got the authority!'

'Then block the goddamn line or something,' Cooper snapped as he started away from the small badly lit office. 'But if that train leaves without me, you'll never live to collect your pension, Howard!'

He made one more stop, woke up Jensen the telegraph operator and ordered him to send an urgent message to the sheriff of Santa Fe.

Have reason to believe Mrs Lu Christmas in grave danger. Request you take her into protective custody. Arriving by Denver train tomorrow. Explain fully then.

> *Chad Cooper, Sheriff*
> *Coldwater, Arizona.*

Jensen looked up from his notebook. 'You ain't sheriff now!'

'Send that message the way I gave it to you,' Cooper ordered and stood over the man to make sure he did.

Then he hurried to his rooming-house, flung a few clothes and a spare box of ammunition into a warbag and started back to the railroad siding.

He was carrying his rifle without its scabbard in his left hand.

Far off in the night he heard the faint, mournful wail of the El Paso–Denver train.

*

Mrs Lu Christmas was a Eurasian. She was a small, thin woman whose beauty of face could not be disguised by the careworn look and the sickness within her.

She moved slowly and gracefully, despite her illness, and her clothes were always impeccable – clean, neat, freshly ironed, and usually of Oriental silk and style. At first she was an object of curiosity in Santa Fe but the town was used to outsiders living amongst them and folks' curiosity soon faded into acceptance. She had been ill when she had arrived with her husband and it was thought that the dry climate would help her respiratory ailment. For a time she improved, high colour in her cheeks, putting on a little weight, but last winter was a severe one and took its toll. She almost died and it was gossiped around town that she needed an expensive operation which would mean her travelling back East.

Everyone knew that Tom Christmas could not afford it and people wondered what would happen to the Eurasian woman. Tom was some kind of a writer – part-time, anyway – spending much of what little money he earned on books for research or sending querying wires across the country asking for information he needed to use in his latest article.

But he looked after Lu well, often taking on odd jobs around town – nothing too menial for him – when he needed extra money for her medicines or treatment such as was offered by the local doctor. On occasion he had brought in other medical people from places like Denver and St Louis.

It had surprised a lot of folk when he had recently sent her off to St Louis – against Lu's objections, knowing they couldn't afford it. But Tom had grinned that boyish way of his and kissed her on the cheek.

'You go, Lu. It's gonna be all right. I've fixed it with Dr Henderson, told him to make arrangements for your operation . . . No, no, don't look scared now! It's gonna be all, right, I promise . . . I've got a deal going right now and I ought to be able to join you in a week and – *presto*! Soon after you'll be a new woman. Now, don't you fret, just do like I say and it'll all be OK . . . I promise.'

She went, but reluctantly, uncertainty mixed with the love she felt for this man she called husband.

They were a couple very much in love and perhaps their affection would carry them through their adversity. But she was the more practical of the two and knew despite what the romance novels said, love could not always conquer everything. . . .

When word reached her that Christmas had been killed down near Coldwater she knew she had been right to doubt him this one time. Her heart like a rock in her breast, she hurried back to Santa Fe. Folk immediately detected a difference in Lu – nothing physical, but there was a new listlessness about her, as if her will to live was diminishing swiftly. Seldom was she seen outside her small house on the north-east edge of town, but when she was, shopping for necessities, more often than not her lovely face was tear-stained and she handed neatly written notes to the storekeepers so as to avoid speaking. Which was a shame because she spoke English well but with that soft, musical lilting of her race that locals found mighty easy on the ears after the rough Western voices they were accustomed to hearing daily.

Now, when Lu Christmas opened her front door, she dabbed genteelly at her moist nostrils and lifted her dark, almond eyes to see who was calling at this hour. They were brimming with tears but they also registered shock when she saw the man who was standing there.

It was Sheriff Hank Keogh. He was a tallish, hard-looking man with beefy shoulders and big scarred hands. His face was rugged but not unkindly and his wide mouth softened a mite now as he doffed his hat, revealing greying, sweat-plastered hair in the lamplight.

'Sorry to disturb you this late, ma'am. Can I come in? Somethin' urgent has come up . . .'

The woman tightened her grip on the edge of the door, the long, slim fingers whitening with the pressure. She took a deep breath and inclined her head, standing to one side, and Keogh eased by, trying not to let his gun-butt brush against her.

She closed the door softly behind her, hurried ahead of him into the parlour, turned up the lamp and offered him a chair and tea. He took the chair but declined the tea.

Her moist eyes sought his and she spoke softly. 'It is more bad news?'

Keogh looked uncomfortable, turned his hat around and around in his big hands, then nodded.

'Afraid it is, ma'am. You can't stay here. You grab

8
Santa Fe

Milt Downey rode through the Pass and left a dust cloud hanging in the air. As soon as he cleared Judas Pass he knew Booker would have him in the lenses of his field glasses.

When the man didn't see Eddie Reid with him he would know something had gone wrong – and Milt wasn't any too keen to explain to Jay Booker just what had happened in Coldwater.

He took the circuitous path through the huge boulder-fields that dotted the barren slope of the range and made for the secret trails that would take him to the outlaw camp.

Downey found his mouth getting drier the closer he drew to the camp and when he rode in and saw the tall, bearded man in gambler-type clothes standing languidly in the shade of one of the few trees that dotted the hidden canyon, Downey felt his bowels quake.

Haskins, of all people! *Christ, as if it wasn't bad enough having to tell Booker . . .*

He dismounted stiffly, coated with dust, the horse standing with drooping head and splayed forelegs, caked with dried yellowish foam.

'Been ridin' hard, Milt,' Booker greeted him from where he sat on a rock, field-glasses beside him, a half-smoked cigarette between nicotine-stained fingers. There was also a small pint-bottle of whiskey, nearly empty; Booker picked it up, took a swig, and rolled it around his mouth before swallowing. 'Damn tooth's still givin' me hell.'

'You shoulda let the dentist pull it while you was there,' Downey said, forcing a grin, trying to sound friendly and untroubled. He glanced sidelong at Haskins, who hadn't moved, the man smoking a cigarillo, looking at his ease. 'Howdy, Mr Haskins, din' 'spect to see you here.'

'Just got in from St Louis this morning. You came back alone.' It wasn't a question, simply a flat statement.

Downey grimaced uncontrollably. He shifted his dusty boots, took off his hat and slapped at his clothes, raising a yellowish haze around him.

'Where's Eddie?' Booker asked, flicking away his cigarette stub and draining the whiskey bottle.

'More to the point,' Haskins said, 'where's this so-called bodyguard Cooper? That's who you were sent to get.'

Downey's belly growled as it rolled nervously. He cleared his throat. 'That Eddie – I know you said no drinkin' before we done the job, Book, but – you know Eddie. He can smell the cork of a whiskey jug three miles off. Place we picked was near the Waterhole saloon. He couldn't resist goin' in to have a few.'

'I knew it!' rapped Booker, sliding down from the rock, his sudden movement causing Downey to take a step backwards. Three other men playing cards outside a crude wickiup under a ledge, paused to watch now. 'Soon as you didn't show last night with Cooper, I knew somethin' had fouled up.'

'Go on, Milt,' the man called Haskins said quietly, but his deep-blue eyes were narrowed and the glint of the sun on them gave them a look like chips of ice. 'Tell it, man.'

Downey wanted to sit down badly, wanted a drink even worse. But he ran a tongue round his lips and said hoarsely, 'Eddie had a grudge agin Cooper – said he nailed his cousin when he was cleanin' up Coldwater. He climbed up on the roof and tried to blow Coop's head off.'

'Jesus Christ!' Booker threw back his head spread his arms and yelled the epithet to the sky, his voice echoing around the canyon.

'He missed and I – I tried to stop him but he went after Cooper and Cooper winged him. Eddie fell down but he was still alive so I – I put two into him.'

Haskins had straightened at Downey's words; now he asked tensely. 'Kill him?'

'Yessir, Mr Haskins. Put 'em into his head – I din' want him talkin' to that Cooper . . .'

'What happened?' Booker asked deceptively, quietly.

'Cooper come after me, but I emptied my rifle at him and hightailed it outta there. Laid up along the trail in case he kept on comin', hopin' I could shoot his hoss out from under him and jump him an' bring him back like you wanted, Mr Haskins . . .'

'But you didn't.'

'No. He – he never come after me. I s'pose by the time he saddled a hoss and so on he must've figured I'd be well away. When I was sure he wasn't comin' I lit out for here. I – I tried my best, Mr Haskins. It was Eddie that fouled things up.'

'Yes – the demon drink has ruined many a man and many a plan,' Haskins agreed slowly. He smiled at Downey. 'I think you handled things as well as you could, Milt, What d'you say, Jay?'

Booker seemed a bit surprised at the man's words, but shrugged. 'If you're happy, boss . . .'

'Who said I was happy?' Haskins asked. 'I merely said I felt Milt had done his best – which was far, far from satisfactory, but the best he was capable of.'

'Then what. . . ?'

The rest of Booker's query was drowned in the blast of the big Smith & Wesson revolver that Haskins produced from beneath his jacket. The slug shattered the startled Downey's face, snapped the man's head back so sharply that his feet actually lifted from the ground before he fell in an inert heap.

The three card-players were on their feet now, staring silently. Booker still looked surprised, but as Haskins turned his cold blue gaze towards him, the outlaw smiled crookedly.

'Yeah,' he said without expression.

Haskins holstered the Smith & Wesson in his spring-clip shoulder-holster, a recent souvenir from St Louis.

'We've wasted enough time, Jay – we'd better get down to Santa Fe. They told me at the St Louis clinic that's where the Chink woman lives. She ran there as soon as she got news about her husband.'

Booker nodded and ordered two of the card players to bury Downey and the third man to saddle his horse and get some grubsacks together.

'How'd you track her to St Louis, boss?' he asked Haskins.

The man smiled and drew on his cigarillo, looking smug. 'I have friends in many places, Jay – even St Louis lung clinics.' Then his voice hardened. 'Now let's *move*! I want that woman before Cooper gets to her.'

It was mid-afternoon when Cooper arrived in Santa Fe and he was the first passenger to drop off the Denver train, hoofing it across the cinders and skirting the white adobe railroad building. He shouldered his warbag, rifle held in his right hand, and hurried uptown, searching for the law-office.

A few folk on the street stopped to stare at the naked gun as he strode along but most gave him a wide berth; his face was set in hard, concentrated lines and it was doubtful that he even saw the people in the bright dry air of this picturesque town.

There were several Indians on the streets and in the plaza, colourful blankets around their shoulders, walking well, not as if they expected to be kicked aside by whites who for some reason might think themselves superior. There was a white-and-terra-cotta trading-post whose sign advertised Indian jewellery, silver-and-turquoise, Navajo and Hopi craft work. At the bottom of the sign were the words: A TRADER HASKINS BUSINESS. Cooper had seen some of his stores in other towns in New Mexico; he was a well-known businessman.

There was a slight haze of dust or smoke over part of the town and just as he sighted the law-office sign, a cedar board with the name burned into the wood swinging on a chain above the doorway, he sniffed and decided it was smoke more than dust.

He turned into the doorway and found a fenced-off section for a reception area with three desks and several cabinets behind. Only one desk was occupied and the man glanced up briefly, then returned to assembling the sixgun he was working on.

'Looking for Sheriff Keogh,' Cooper said.

'That so.' The deputy didn't look up.

'My name's Cooper. I sent him a wire yesterday.'

The man looked up now, a young, cocky face with a beginning moustache – an attempt to make him look older.

'So you're the one stirred up all the trouble.' His voice had a nasty edge to it.

'Trouble? I asked the sheriff to . . .'

'*Know* what you asked him!' the deputy cut in harshly, eyes boring into the dusty man at the railings. He looked him up and down arrogantly and didn't seem to care much for what he saw. 'So you're the famous Chad Cooper – "Coop".' He managed to make the name sound like something a man would want to spit out pronto. He stood tall and big, but a lot of it was flab and mostly around his middle. He hitched at a gunbelt, twin holsters, only one filled now. Presumably the gun on his desk was the missing weapon.

'The hired gun who passes himself off as a lawman.'

'Where'll I find the sheriff, sonny?' Cooper asked tiredly.

The 'sonny' did not go down well with the deputy. He started around his desk towards the rail. Cooper set down his warbag and held up his hand.

'If you're thinking what I think you're thinking, *sonny*, my advice is to forget it. Right now – just tell me where Keogh is.'

'Why, you two-bit tinhorn! You don't count for nothing with me!' The deputy came swiftly, kicking open the swinging gate and stepping right up to Cooper, lifting his gun, ready to club the man.

Cooper kicked him savagely in the shins and the man's face crumpled in pain and shock. He staggered back, dropping his gun. Cooper grabbed one of the big flabby arms, put it up between the man's shoulders and bent him over the fence. He stood back and kicked the well-padded backside, releasing his hold so that the deputy slid over the rail and sprawled on the floor on the other side.

'What the hell's goin' on here?'

Cooper turned, the rifle he still held kind of floating around casually to cover the big man now filling the street doorway. He caught the glint of sunlight on the brass of the sheriff's star pinned to the shirt-pocket.

'Just returning your deputy's greeting, Keogh. He's not a man you ought to have in your front office.'

Keogh looked past Cooper to where his deputy was getting up, rubbing at his shin, a scrape of flesh hanging from one of his cheeks.

'You actin' tough again, Lonnie?'

'Aw, he smart-mouthed me, Hank! I was just gonna make sure he knew we don't aim to treat him like a real lawman.'

Keogh grunted, looked at Cooper. 'Lonnie tries hard – my sister's boy. Father died when he was a shaver and I kinda helped bring him up. Looks up to me.'

'You didn't teach him good enough manners.'

Keogh's eyes narrowed. 'Well, that makes no nevermind – Lonnie's my problem. You've got bigger ones.'

Keogh shouldered past Cooper, held open the swinging gate and jerked his head for Cooper to follow. The gunfighter picked up his warbag and Lonnie glared as he went past.

'Go take a walk round town, Lon – show the badge,' ordered the sheriff and the deputy quickly grabbed a hat from a wall peg, picked up his dropped Colt and went out, ramming the gun into his holster. He seemed happy enough to leave.

Keogh sat down at his desk and gestured to the visitor's chair which Cooper sank into.

'Lu Christmas,' he said, eyes hard.

Keogh took off his hat, ran thick fingers through his damp hair and sighed. 'Yeah – poor old China Lu – that's what they call her in town now.'

Cooper frowned. 'Why?'

'She's a Chinee. Din' you know?'

Cooper shook his head. 'Don't make any difference. You got my wire, according to Lonnie. You take her into protective custody?'

Keogh was rolling a cigarette, pushed the makings across the desk but Cooper shook his head, his gaze not leaving the sheriff's face. He watched the lawman hunt around for a match, then fumble lighting it a few times before he got his smoke going.

Delaying, Cooper thought, tensing up now.

Keogh leaned back in his chair, big yellow teeth tugging at his lower lip.

'Too late,' he said heavily.

'What? You didn't take her into protective custody?'

'Oh, sure. I brought her in all right, fixed up a cell for her real nice. But she walked out.'

Cooper didn't believe what he was hearing and his rugged face showed it. 'Who'd you have on duty?' he asked softly. 'Lonnie?'

The sheriff looked a mite uncomfortable. 'Kid tries hard. Got a lot to learn and hasn't really sorted himself out yet. She said she was cold and her cough was bothering her. Asked him to go fetch her a warmer jacket and bottle of some Chinee herbs medicine from the house. When he got back she was gone.'

'He never locked the cell door when he left?'

The lawman shrugged. 'Hell, I dunno – he was just tryin' to be obligin'. But what's it matter? She's gone and I haven't been able to find her.'

'That don't surprise me any. You look?'

Keogh coloured, his face tightening. 'Now you watch your mouth! 'Course we damn well looked!'

'I'll bet. You and Lonnie both, huh? If Lonnie learns from you, I can figure out just how hard you looked for a Chinee woman some hired gun asked you to hold for him.'

Keogh leaned across his desk. 'Yeah? Well, why don't *you* look for her? I don't owe you nothin', Cooper: you ain't even a real lawman – fact, you *cheapen* an honourable trade, hirin' out your gun and pinnin' on a sheriff's star just like anyone hauled in off the street. It ain't right.'

'What you know about honour you can stick in a gnat's rear end, Keogh.'

'By hell!' Hank Keogh jumped to his feet, face almost purple now, breath hissing through wide nostrils. 'I oughta throw you outta my town! Instead, I'll do you one last favour, and it *will be* the last. Mebbe you can still smell the smoke.'

'What?' Cooper frowned, caught off-balance by the sudden remark.

The sheriff grinned crookedly. 'China Lu's place burned down last night. She might even a done it herself – I dunno and I don't care. She's your problem, Cooper, all yours!'

9
China Doll

The ruins of the house on Blackwood Street were still smouldering a little when Cooper arrived.

They smelled of smoke and water and steam and there were a couple of kids poking around but they ran off, giving cheeky gestures, when Chad Cooper appeared.

The place must have been pretty small, likely with only one or two bedrooms and single-storeyed. Everything had collapsed or burned up. There didn't appear to be anything worth salvaging or that *could* be salvaged. Cooper wandered around in the gathering dusk, hearing the whistle of a train coming out of the snaking pass through the Sangre De Cristo mountains. A few people looked at him curiously but no one wandered over for a closer look. A fire always drew crowds of scavengers and the plain nosy but apparently most folk had already seen all they wanted to – or salvaged what interested them, even if it didn't belong to them.

One house to the right of the ruins had scorch marks and a couple of heat-cracked windows but the fire seemed to have been contained mostly in the Christmases' lot. Cooper didn't know why he had come here, really – just to see it for himself, maybe, but what that would accomplish he didn't know.

Locating Lu Christmas was the priority. If she was still around, she was in danger. Booker or his pards could easily turn up here, searching for her, and if they got their hands on her she would surely suffer, whether she knew anything about her husband's package or not. They would take lots of convincing that she was just an innocent in this.

Even Cooper didn't know whether she *was* innocent.

But the danger part was real enough, always supposing Booker or whoever was in the photograph figured it important enough to make sure no more prints existed.

Which might, in turn, put Rosa Cisco in danger, too!

Hell, why hadn't he thought of that earlier!

They would know the picture was part of the big panorama Rosa had shot, so sooner or later they were going to go back to her because she was the only one with the original plates. *Damn, but he was handling this in a sloppy manner!* He had let his disappointment at the loss of the bonus throw his concentration. If he didn't pull his socks up pronto he was going to get someone else killed! And for all he knew, Lu Christmas might already be dead.

That wasn't a pleasant thought but he had just

decided there was nothing to be gained here and started to turn away when something stopped him dead in his tracks.

A sound.

But what the hell was it? And where did it come from? He stood very still, listening, trying to blot out the sounds of the town and the birds homing in the dusk.

There it was again!

But *what* was it? Some sort of animal? Must be. It resembled a muffled cough. He turned this way and that, trying to get a direction.

He frowned. It appeared to be coming from over to his left but he could see only criss-crossed, badly burned timbers there, resting on the scorched flooring where they had fallen during the fire. There wasn't enough room for any animal to hide there. Then he heard it again and he slowly walked across, moving some of the timbers, looking at the floor which was mostly hidden beneath a thick layer of ash and charred wood. Just as he started to kick some aside he heard the sound once more.

Almost beneath where he was standing!

Cooper scraped some ash and rubbish to one side, and saw the dirt-filled crack in the floorboards. A trapdoor!

Root cellar! He began heaving beams and general rubbish to one side. In moments he had revealed the trapdoor, pulled out his hunting-knife and used the heavy blade to work down into the crack through the clogging dirt. He levered up enough of the door edge for him to grip with his fingers and pulled it open, choking in a cloud of ash and dust.

The coughing below came loud and distinct now and he clawed his eyes clear in time to see what he thought was a child clambering up the ladder towards him, coughing wrackingly, head hidden by a scarf. He grabbed one groping small hand and heaved.

As she sprawled – he could see the soiled dress now, burned ragged in places – gleaming jet-black hair spilled out from under the scarf and he glimpsed one almond-shaped eye and smeared marble-like skin.

'Mrs Christmas?' he asked incredulously.

She started to reply but another fit of coughing caught her and her small body shook as the spasms wracked her. Her eyes were wide as she studied him, cramming a handkerchief over her mouth. It was plain she was mighty leery of this stranger. He tried to calm her.

'I'm Chad Cooper, ma'am – the man Tom hired to ride with him to Judas Pass . . .'

She lowered the handkerchief, shuddered with two diminishing coughs, then spoke, her voice hoarse from smoke.

'You are the one who did not protect him!'

'Well, I guess that's true, but there's a little more to it, ma'am. You see, Tom played it down, said it wasn't really dangerous, that he needed me to guide him to the Pass as much as anything . . . I was caught napping when the shooting started.' He added quickly, 'I'm not trying to make excuses, and I'm here to tell you I feel mighty bad about it all, but –

well, that can wait. We've got to get you out of here.'

She pulled back as he reached for her, at the same time looking around to see if anyone was watching. But there was no one right now and he figured folk were hurrying home for supper as darkness descended, bringing a chill with it. He saw Lu hugging herself, heard the chattering of her teeth and gave her his denim jacket, feeling her thinness as he wrapped it about her shoulders.

'Why were you hiding in the root cellar?' he asked suddenly. 'Fire catch you unawares?'

She rolled her eyes towards him and didn't answer right away. 'No – I started the fire myself. I hid down in the cellar, thinking no one would ever look for me there beneath the ruins of a burned-out building, but I did not expect so much smoke – I was sure they must hear me coughing but in all the noise of trying to put the fire out they apparently did not and I was not discovered. Then when I tried to open the trapdoor, I couldn't move it.'

'Some beams had fallen across it,' he said, realizing just how desperate this frightened little woman must have felt to pull off such a thing. 'You're lucky you didn't die down there.'

Again those disconcerting eyes sought his face. 'It would not have mattered. Now that Tom is gone . . . You are the one who sent me the message to say he was dead?'

Cooper nodded, leading her carefully over the rubble, still watching the street and other houses. 'We buried him in Coldwater, ma'am. I hope that was all right.'

She surprised him when he felt the sudden pressure of her slim fingers against his hand. 'I am grateful, Mr Cooper ... I think perhaps if Tom had confided in you more he might still be alive.'

'I'd like to think so, ma'am.' But he felt that she had decided to accept him as an ally rather than an enemy.

Now they had to get out of here – 'here' being Santa Fe itself – while they still had a chance. There was only one place to go, of course – Coldwater.

And it was a long way from here. . . .

'So you found her after all!'

Cooper jumped and instinctively thrust the woman away from him, causing her to stumble and give a small cry of alarm. He swung up the rifle but paused with it held in both hands as he saw Deputy Lonnie standing there, Colt menacing.

'Uh-uh, gunfighter! I got the drop this time – and I can shoot you down easy and Uncle Hank won't even bother to ask for an explanation!'

Cooper shrugged, let the rifle barrel sag groundwards, leaning down to steady Lu Christmas as she staggered to her feet. 'You all right, ma'am?'

'Yes, thank you ...' Then she smiled at Lonnie. 'The obliging deputy ...'

'Don't you try to bamboozle me with that smile no more, China Lu! You got me in a lotta trouble with my uncle.'

'I am sorry, Lonnie. But I was afraid to stay in jail.'

'Heck, I was gonna take care of you, I told you.'

'Yes, Lonnie, but I did not feel safe. If someone was going to come for me, then where could I go? Where could I hide, if I was in jail? All they had to do was come and collect me. I was desperate. I had to get out.'

Lonnie scratched his head. 'Well, no one woulda gotten to you while I was on duty. I—'

Cooper swung the rifle suddenly and knocked the Colt out of Lonnie's hand, the barrel clanging briefly. The sixgun leapt wildly, spinning as it struck Lonnie in the chest. He fell to one knee, clawing at himself. The woman cried out, ducked low, and grabbed at Cooper.

He disengaged her hand and took a step forward, knocking Lonnie on to his side with the rifle-barrel.

'Don't hurt him! Please!'

Cooper raised his eyebrows at Lu then shrugged and even helped the dazed deputy to a sitting position. Lonnie rubbed at his head, blinked up at Cooper.

'Don't you never hit anyone with your goddamn fists!'

'Not if I can help it, Lonnie – I'm a gunfighter and a man's hands are the slowest thing to heal after a fist-fight, don't you know that? Sore hands don't make for a fast draw.'

Lonnie blinked. 'I never thought of that . . . What you gonna do with me?'

'Tie you up or knock you out. We have to be going and we need a decent start.'

Lonnie looked from one to the other. 'What you runnin' from?'

'Not sure, to tell you the truth,' Cooper admitted. 'But I think the men who killed Tom Christmas are gonna come after Lu.'

The deputy shifted his gaze to the Chinese woman. 'That right, ma'am?'

'I am not sure . . .'

'Well, I think mebbe Coop's right,' Lonnie said, heaving to his feet. As they stared at him, he added, 'Hank sent me down here to see if you'd found Lu. He got an urgent telegraph message after you'd left that stirred him up.'

'What sort of message? And who from?'

'Well, Hank just said – in a kinda panic, like – "*We gotta find that China Lu, Lon! Haskins is comin' himself an' he wants me to have her waitin'.*" '

'*Trader* Haskins?' asked Cooper, unable to keep the surprise out of his voice.

'Yeah – Uncle Hank kinda keeps an eye on his tradin' post and does an odd job or two for him when he wants him to.'

'What kind of odd jobs?'

Lonnie looked away, shrugged awkwardly. 'That's between Mr Haskins and Uncle Hank – he don't tell me the details but I know Hank gets paid well, Sometimes he tosses me a few extra bucks . . .'

'Well, I dunno Haskins from spit – what's he like?'

Lonnie didn't really want to talk about Haskins but said, 'Well, he seems OK. Smiles a lot, always polite to womenfolk – has one of them close-cut beards that come to a point, gives him a narrow look. But his eyes – his eyes are real scary. He looks more of a – killer than you do.'

'You heard of him killing anyone?'

Lonnie shook his head. 'I – I don't like to ask

much about him. I try to be outta town whenever he
shows up.'

'Well, I can't take any chances if he wants Mrs
Christmas held till he gets here – which will be when?
You know?'

'Comin' in on the night train from Albuquerque.'

Cooper remembered the distant whistle he had
heard. 'That'll be pulling in any time! Sorry, Lon.
Got nothing to tie you up with, so . . .' He raised the
rifle-barrel and Lonnie cowered back lifting a hand
protectively.

'Wait!' he almost yelled. 'I can get you a coupla
hosses. Show you a safe way outta town.'

Cooper held the blow he had been about to
deliver, still undecided. 'Why would you do that?' he
asked.

'Aw, I dunno – Hank's kind of a strange feller at
times, makes me do things I don't want to. Besides I
– I always liked – her.' He flushed as he indicated Lu
Christmas. 'She always said "hello" and didn' make
fun of me like the others if I was clumsy or messed up
somethin' I was doin' . . .' He lowered his eyes,
embarrassed.

'Thank you, Lonnie,' Lu said, smiling warmly.

Cooper lowered the rifle. 'Lonnie, I believe there's
hope for you yet.'

Cooper heard it as soon as they led the horses out of
the stables behind the darkened law-office: the
hollow panting of a train at the siding. He turned to
look at Lonnie and the deputy compressed his lips
and nodded.

'That's the Albuquerque train. Come all the way from St Louis. We better get started.'

Lu Christmas did not look happy about the prospect of riding all the way back to Coldwater, but she remained silent. Lonnie led the way out of a gate in the rear fence, sweating, hoping his uncle had gone to meet the train. He was afoot and his heart was hammering as he led Cooper and the girl, both still unmounted, along a weed-grown path that petered out at the edge of town where the Rio began. This far north the river was less muddy than down along the border but it was also deeper and the woman seemed frightened at the idea of swimming her horse across.

'You'll be all right, ma'am,' Lonnie assured her, sounding breathless, looking about him constantly, nervous as a bride. 'I better be gettin' back – Uncle Hank'll be lookin' for me.'

Cooper swung into the saddle and Lonnie turned to help Lu. She was clumsy and obviously nervous and the horse sensed it, snorted and started to move its feet back and forth.

'Get him into the water quick as you can,' advised Cooper. 'Lonnie – I won't forget this. You take some advice, you'll find yourself another job, away from Keogh.'

Lonnie didn't answer, just started jog-trotting back along the path towards the rear of the law-office.

Cooper put his mount alongside Lu's, reached out for her horse's bridle and urged both animals into the river.

He heard her gasp as the water slid up her legs

and she started to move as if she would slide out of the saddle.

'Calm down, dammit!' he hissed. 'It's not all that far and once we're across we're clear and can head south. Might even be able to pick up a stage to Coldwater coming north from Socorro, according to Lonnie.'

'I do not like rivers! My mother and two sisters were drowned in a flood . . .' She was having trouble breathing and he knew he was going to have his work cut out handling her this night – and maybe all the other nights before they reached Coldwater.

He sighed.

'OK. But just listen to me – *listen*! I've crossed a couple of hundred rivers under all conditions and I'm still alive and kicking. Do like I say and you'll be all right.' He took her thin arm and shook her, startling her. 'You understand, Lu? *Do – like – I – say*! No more, no less. OK?'

Her almond eyes bulging, she nodded, the reins cutting into her fine hands as she tightened her grip.

'Good. Then let's . . .'

Someone shouted but the sound was drowned out by the crash of a rifle and water leapt between the horses as the bullet zipped into the river. Cooper jammed in the spurs, slapped his hat across the jerking head of the woman's mount and they plunged into the muddy waters.

More bullets splashed and zipped around them and the girl clung awkwardly, almost lying along the horse's back. Cooper flicked his rifle free of the scabbard, jammed the reins between his teeth and levered a shell into the breech. He hipped in the saddle and saw three or four men on the riverbank, all were afoot. He couldn't be sure, but he didn't think Lonnie was one of them.

He was right about that.

When Lonnie had returned to the law-office yard he had seen the group of men milling about by the stables. He had been seen so it was far too late to run back through the gate. He had to brazen it out and his bowels quaked when he found that the group comprised Hank Keogh, Trader Haskins, Jay Booker, and two hardcases named Deke and Lew.

'Lon!' the sheriff barked when he was sure it was his nephew and he saw the others lower their guns. 'Where the hell're the hosses?'

'Er – I dunno, Hank – I was inside and thought I heard somethin' out here and when I come out I seen both our hosses was gone. I started out the gate towards the river to look for them but heard you so I came back.'

'You see who took the broncs?' snapped Trader Haskins. Lonnie had never liked the man and wished he had had time to work out a story that would sound believable. Instead, he cleared his throat nervously and said, 'Dunno, Mr Haskins – I never got a look at 'em before I come runnin' back here.'

Haskins looked hard at the boy in the dim light and although Lonnie couldn't make out the dreaded eyes he squirmed uncomfortably. Keogh started to speak but Haskins held up a hand, stopping him. He stroked his close-cropped beard, drawing it to a point almost absently.

'You're lyin', kid,' he said gently and Lonnie shook his head vigorously, unable to speak at that moment.

'Easy, now,' cut in the sheriff, although he, too, could tell his nephew was lying. 'Lon needs time to think these kinda things through, Trader—'

'It was Cooper, wasn't it?' snapped Haskins, ignoring Keogh. 'And if he took both horses it means the Chinee woman's with him. The hell're you playin' at, kid?'

While they were talking, the man called Lew had gone out through the gate and run along the path to the river. He appeared again now as Lonnie croaked in a scared voice,

'Listen, I never seen who it was! Gospel, Mr Haskins . . .'

'Trader!' called Lew, 'Two people swimmin' their hosses across the river!'

Haskins rounded on the startled Lonnie, whose crumbling face gave him away and before he stepped back quickly, the boy stammered, 'He couldn'ta seen 'em! They was further upstream . . .'

'But there're currents to bring 'em downstream, too, you dummy!' growled Haskins and his Smith & Wesson appeared from under his left arm and blasted the night apart.

Lonnie was hurled back by the impact, his hat jerking off, gasped as he clawed at his chest and went down, rolling around briefly before he was still.

'Christ almighty!' choked Keogh and ran to kneel beside his nephew, pulling Lonnie's head on to his knees, stroking the sweat-soaked curls. He turned an anguished face towards Haskins. 'Goddamnit, you din' have to do that!'

Haskins wasn't interested, started moving towards the gate, his men following. 'Hurry it up before they get away!'

Keogh felt sick as he watched Lonnie die in his arms, trying vainly to say something.

Now, in midstream, Cooper lifted his rifle and triggered. Suddenly there were only three men still on their feet on the riverbank. The fourth thrashed in the coarse sand only briefly before being still.

The others scattered and Cooper hurried them along with four more swift shots.

Lu's horse was acting up, plunging, the water frothing, and she screamed briefly before she fell. Cooper rammed his rifle back into its scabbard as he dived off his own horse, reaching for her as her frail arms flapped wildly and she started to sink. His groping fingers found the long hair and he yanked her head above water. She coughed and gagged as he slid an arm around her and grabbed at his horse's mane. The animal swam strongly, experienced in river crossings, going with the current a little, angling across when safe to do so.

The men on shore were shooting again now but the fugitives were too far away and too low in the water to make good targets in this light.

Cooper knew that getting out on the far bank would be the dangerous part and he threw his weight on his mount's mane, pulling its head around, forcing it to swim downstream towards some overhanging bushes. The girl was gagging and thrashing wildly, a few of her unaimed blows catching him on the ear and face. Her riderless mount was whinnying and striking the water with its hoofs but it instinctively followed Cooper's horse.

Then the bushes were between them and the men shooting at them and Cooper released the mane and struck out for the bank with Lu. His feet touched bottom after a few strokes and he fell once, dragging the terrified woman under. But he lifted her in his arms, found his footing and, dripping, fought his way up the bank. He laid her down on the ground, breathing hard, as the horses heaved out of the water, shook themselves and immediately began browsing on the grass.

Cooper turned the woman on to her face and pressed his hands against her lower ribs, squeezing, half afraid he might break something, she seemed so fragile.

She coughed and spat water and a little sand, began to shiver, hugging herslf.

'We need to get moving fast. Soon as I figure it's safe I'll light a fire and get you dried out. Savvy?'

She stared back at him dully, then after another moment, nodded. 'Thank you,' she whispered, ever polite.

On the far bank, Trader Haskins lowered his hot rifle and turned to Jay Booker beside him. 'We have to have horses.'

'I'll get some, even if I have to shoot the livery

man,' Booker said and moved away into the darkness. 'Pick you up back at the law-office.'

The third survivor was kneeling beside the man Cooper had shot. 'Lew's kin of mine, Mr H – all right if I bury him?'

'Certainly, Deke – if you want to be laid alongside him,' Haskins said grimly as the other man started. 'He's dead. We're here to stop Cooper and the Chink woman. That's our priority. Now let's get back to the law-office.'

Reluctantly, Deke left the body. Haskins pushed him impatiently back towards Santa Fe. In the law-office, they found Hank Keogh in the living-quarters at the back. He was standing beside the bed where he had laid out Lonnie's body.

He looked coldly at Trader Haskins and Deke. 'He was only a boy!' he said. 'A bit dumb, but a pretty good kid.'

Haskins shrugged, plainly uninterested. He poured himself a drink from an open whiskey bottle and Deke did the same.

'He brought it on himself . . .'

Keogh started to argue but he knew Haskins was right. It didn't make Lonnie's murder any easier to take, though. He sighed and stared down at the dead face. The kid looked peaceful enough. Hank Keogh had done his best for him after his sister's husband had died but – he had to admit it – Lonnie hadn't been very smart and sooner or later it was bound to get him killed. But Haskins had shot him with no more thought than swatting a fly; that was what was annoying him. *That wasn't right . . .*

Hank Keogh might not have lived up to his oath of office all the time but he knew how a man had to act in certain situations. And this one could be settled only one way. . . .

'Trader!'

Haskins must have been expecting it. He had transferred his whiskey glass to his left hand and now as he turned to face the lawman, his right hand was already closing about the butt of the Smith & Wesson in its shoulder holster. He smiled thinly as he saw Keogh crouched, hand poised above his sixgun butt, ready to fight and avenge his stupid nephew.

'Ah, Hank, I always knew you were a fool!' Haskins said and shot the lawman casually as Keogh's gun started to lift.

Keogh went down hard, sitting on his folded legs beside the bed that held Lonnie. He tried to bring up the gun but it was way too heavy for him. A little blood showed at the corner of his mouth as his chin sagged forward on to his chest with infinite slowness, dripping red.

Haskins downed his drink and jerked his head at Deke and they started for the door, hearing Booker calling from out in the street that he had mounts for everyone now.

Neither looked back.

10
Trailside

Cooper had always had an instinct for direction. It had gotten him out of trouble many times in the past and he hoped it would stand by him this night.

Lonnie had drawn a crude map of how to follow the river valley once across and then find a way through the low-slung Bandolier range before making a swing south to the smaller Rio Puerces. It was a long way and led through old cliff dwellings of the fabled Anastasi and pueblo ruins. Lonnie had said it was country that he liked and that whenever he could get away from his duties as deputy he would make for this place and spend a day or two just wandering around the eerie clay dwellings.

Strange lad, Cooper thought. Not too bright but he had a lot of good healthy curiosity. Now Cooper tried to recall that crude map in his mind as he led the mostly silent Chinese woman along the little-used trails. The cough of a mountain lion brought her riding in close enough for their legs to touch, but she seemed to relax when he unshipped his rifle and rode with it across his thighs.

By luck or by instinct – he wasn't sure which – he found the cliff dwellings, took the south swing and that brought him into the sandy basin at the foot of other cliffs where pueblo ruins showed dimly in the starlight.

'We can build a fire there,' he said, although she was mostly dried out now, but the cough was troubling her and he figured a little extra warmth wouldn't hurt.

They found a cosy section, mostly intact, but he had to chase out a coiled snake which upset her a little. He didn't let her see the hairy tarantula that he squashed under his boot – and made out he was merely stamping his foot because it had gone numb while he was gathering firewood. He built a small fire, heated beans and insisted she eat while he brewed some coffee that made her grimace, it was so strong.

But she curled up in a corner on the blankets and he settled with his saddle for a pillow, tilted his hat over his eyes and laid the rifle across his lap.

Both were soon asleep

He didn't know how much later it was that something woke him up but he came out of shallow sleep, rolling on to one knee, the rifle coming around in both hands, thumb notching back the hammer, finger on the trigger. He saw the moving shadow against one wall and his finger tightened. He paused as the shadow took a lurching step forward and then collapsed on to one knee, a hand reaching out to steady its owner against the adobe wall. The battered hat fell off and in the glow of the fire's coals he recognized Sheriff Hank Keogh.

The man looked at him out of reddened, sunken eyes and there was dried blood at the corner of his mouth. A towel had been tied around his body just above his waist in the form of a crude bandage. Dark patches showed through.

Cooper went to him, laid him out gently but still the big lawman grunted in pain. Lu Christmas's eyes flew open but she didn't move her head or any other part of her body: just her almond eyes, watching as Cooper gave Keogh a drink from his canteen. The sheriff was breathing harshly.

'You alone?' Cooper asked and for a moment he thought the lawman tried to smile.

'Cagey, ain't you? Yeah, I'm – alone – Haskins killed Lonnie – tried to square with him but – he's way too fast – underarm – the left one – if you ever run – up against him.'

'Thanks, I'll remember that. And you can rest easy, Keogh. I *will* run into Trader Haskins. I promise you that.'

Keogh's head nodded loosely. 'He's – ridin' for Coldwater – with Booker and – feller named Deke. All killers – I beat 'em here 'cause I knew if – Lonnie helped you he'd tell you about this shortcut through the Bandoliers – his favourite country . . .' His mind seemed to wander and the focus of his eyes changed as he shook his head slowly. 'Never figured Haskins'd turn on – me – but . . .'

'Lonnie said you worked for him sometimes.'

'Yeah – easy money – kinda bent the law some, but not – too bad . . .'

'All I ever heard about Haskins was that he was a mighty sharp businessman, had several trading posts and stores around the south-west . . . Never heard of him being a killer or fast with a gun.'

'You would've – if you knew his real name . . . Larry Bergen.'

Cooper let that sink in as Keogh took another swallow of water. Yeah, he had heard of Bergen. Mostly up north in the Dakotas or Montana. Some said he came from Canada, and was once leader of a highly successful gang of train robbers. The law had had him in its hands on several occasions but he had either escaped or hired some sharp lawyer who got him off on a technicality.

'Haven't heard of him in years,' Cooper said but for some reason immediately thought of the post-script on the bottom of Pete Gilbert's letter to Tom Christmas. It had said: *You know who to see about 'B' – bad cess to the s.o.b.*

Could that 'B' have stood for Bergen? Gilbert was a journalist known for his fearless exposes. It could be possible.

'Yeah, well, he's been kinda – quiet – these past five or six years,' Keogh went on, fighting for breath now. 'Took the "Trader Haskins" name but stayed in touch with old gang members and now and again used them on some job he figured out was just too good to pass up . . .'

Cooper stared hard down at the dying lawman.

'Have to ask how you knew him, Keogh.'

The lawman managed a crooked smile. 'Can't you figure? When Lonnie's father died and I had to be responsible for bringin' him up and lookin' after my sister, I knew I was gonna need more money than my job of ridin' shotgun on the stages brought in. So I set him up with a coupla payroll runs – for a percentage.' He tried to sneer but a coughing fit caught him and it was some time before he could continue.

'I sort of got religion after that and took on a lawman's badge. But when Haskins needed somethin' I could give him – well, he just come and seen me or sent someone like Booker to see me and remind me of my past . . .'

'That's the way it goes, I guess. You know anything about the Tom Christmas deal?'

The sheriff was silent for a time. 'Not much – except it's set Haskins off. He's gonna kill you and the Chinee woman if he ever catches up with you.'

'Why did you come here, Hank? You would've been better off seeing a sawbones in Santa Fe.'

Keogh shook his head. 'No – I know bullet wounds. He got me good. I'm through – but I – I just didn't want him to get away with killin' poor Lonnie the way he did. But I'll tell you one thing – he's up to somethin'. I dunno just what but he come to me and *asked* me to arrest him and stick him in my jail, way back at the end of June, I recollect.'

That threw Cooper. He blinked, stirred the fire a little, bringing more light into the shadowy room.

'He *asked* you to throw him in jail?'

Keogh nodded and Cooper had to give him several gentle shakes to bring him back. 'Huh .. ? Yeah. Wanted me to make out that there was a Wanted dodger with a description on it – no picture – that could've fitted him. Funny, it was for a feller named Steed, wanted for several train robberies . . .'

Cooper shook his head. 'What the hell was Haskins playing at?'

'You got me – and wait'll you hear the next part – he had me release him on the quiet for a few days in July. One of his own men took his place in the jail, din' look a helluva lot like him but he dressed in his clothes and so on and if anyone asked for the prisoner I could produce one. But where Haskins went, and what he did, I dunno. But I think Tom Christmas . . .' He stopped speaking suddenly, grimacing, grabbing at the bloody patch on his towel bandage, looking up into Cooper's face with wide, fear-filled eyes,. 'Just – get – H – Ha . . .'

He groped for Cooper's hand and his grip was strong – but only for a short time. It loosened abruptly and Keogh fell back with one final, harsh sigh, head lolling, eyes still wide and staring.

Cooper closed them with thumb and finger and, grim-faced, said quietly, 'I'll get him, Hank. For you, for Lonnie, and most of all for Tom Christmas.'

When he looked over to the corner, he met Lu's steady almond gaze. He thought he saw a touch of fear in those eyes.

Fear of Chad Cooper.

They picked up a stage to Coldwater north-west of

Socorro, turning loose the mounts that Lonnie had supplied.

The Chinese woman was not well received by the other passengers already on the coach, maybe because her clothes were tattered and filthy from the fire and the river. No one met Cooper's gaze for long: they flicked their eyes in his direction, took one look at his hard, challenging face and turned back to the windows in a hurry. He made a point of putting one arm about Lu so she could rest her head against him and catch up on some sleep. Now and again she coughed without waking up. This, too, did nothing to make the other passengers accept her more readily.

'Chinee is she?' asked a heavy-jowled man in a seat opposite Cooper. He had earlier said he sold snake-oil and 'the Good Lord's natural medicaments . . .'

Cooper stared back without answering. The man smiled.

'Knew one in a – well, a *place*.' He winked heavily and knowingly at Cooper, man to man. 'You know. Man, I figured I might move in and live there. Never had such . . .'

Cooper kicked the door open, grabbed the man's shirtfront and without a word, threw him out of the moving stagecoach. The drummer yelled and then thudded to the soft earth at the edge of the trail as the stage laboured up a grade. He rolled and floundered and, coughing, rose to his knees, beginning to panic when he saw the stage drawing away.

He staggered to his feet and began to lurch after it, waving and calling hoarsely. Before Cooper closed the door again, he leaned out and spoke to the driver who was cussing a bluey streak

'No use askin' me to stop, cowboy!' the driver said. 'Never get the team started again we stop on this grade. Damn idiot. He oughta know better'n to lean against the door.'

'Must've dozed off,' called back Cooper innocently. 'He'll be all right. Shackleton is only a few miles east of this trail. He'll be there by sundown.'

'Gonna make paperwork for me,' the driver griped.

'He'll be wantin' a refund.'

Cooper just waved and settled back in his seam, closing the door and rearranging Lu's position: she had not woken up during the brief drama. The other passengers looked mighty leery of Cooper who gave a crooked grin and shrugged.

'Mighty clumsy feller,' he opined and no one contradicted him.

It was early morning before the stage arrived in Coldwater, barely daylight, and few folk were moving about. Cooper left Lu sitting in the stage company waiting-room and went to shake Feeney awake where he was snoring in the bunk he had moved into his office at the rear of the stables.

Feeney blinked in the light of the lantern burning on his desk, rubbed his eyes and shook his head as if he was trying to shake off a bad dream. He moaned.

'Judas! I thought we'd seen the last of you!'

'Back like a bad penny, Feen. Don't look so worried. All I want to know is if three men have come in last night or during the last few hours.' He described Haskins, Booker and Deke as well as he could, figuring they could not have reached Coldwater yet, but there was just a chance they might have picked up an earlier stage from Socorro or Albuquerque.

Feeney shook his head. 'I ain't had no one come in except for local cowhands since last night. Gospel, Coop!'

Cooper believed him but didn't soften the hard set to his mouth. 'You find me and let me know soon as they stable their mounts, Feeno. And do it pronto once they're here.'

Feeney nodded, still wary. 'What – sure, whatever you say, Coop. Glad to help out.'

'Don't overdo it, Feeney,' Cooper said as he left. He went back to the stage depot, picked up Lu and took her to see Doc Peebles.

He waited while the medic examined her and gave her some medicine for the cough. Peebles spoke quietly to Cooper while Lu was getting dressed.

'Developing lung fever unless I miss my guess. See she takes the medicine and gets plenty of rest and good food.' He paused and squinted at Cooper. 'I take it you *are* playing the Good Samaritan and looking out for her?'

'Got no choice, it seems, Doc – that's Tom Christmas's wife.'

'Oh – well, I know she'll be in good hands with you. But if that cough gets any worse or she spits up any blood, you get her back to me right away. You'll have to find somewhere quiet for her, Chad. She's pretty bad and going to get worse if she doesn't have the right attention.'

'Couldn't you. . . ?'

Peebles shook his head before Cooper could complete the question. 'Sorry – wife's down in Tucson, the nurse I have for the infirmary is only part-time.'

Cooper sighed. 'OK – I dunno how I get myself in these binds, but I'll find somewhere.'

Peebles smiled. 'You enjoy it, Chad! You try to hide it but deep down you enjoy it. This is penance for letting Tom get killed, isn't it?'

'Ah, go to hell, you broken-down sawbones! What would you know?' Cooper stomped out and Peebles chuckled.

Rosa Cisco's brown eyes narrowed and she stood looking hard at Cooper in her darkroom which, not being in use at present, was ablaze with white lamplight.

'What makes you think I have any nursing ability, Cooper! You've got a damn cheek asking me to care for that Chinee woman!'

'Yeah, I know. But she only needs rest and good grub and has to take Doc Peebles' medicines on time, that's all. Nothing much to ask, Rosa. Also, she'll be safer here than in one of the rooming-houses.'

'Safer? Safe from what? Haskins and his gang?'

Cooper stiffened. 'What d'you know about Haskins?'

Rosa couldn't resist a superior smile. 'I'd hazard a

guess and say more than you do.'

He was still puzzled. 'I never knew he was in it until I went to Santa Fe, so how could you. . . ?'

'I guessed,' she said, maddeningly off-hand.

'Well, you couldn't've pulled a guess like that out of the air. What the hell's been happening since I went to Santa Fe?'

She turned to face him, still smiling. 'You know that notebook you gave me. . . ?'

'Tom Christmas's? Sure . . .'

She shook her head. 'It wasn't Tom's. It belonged to Peter Gilbert who apparently sent it to Tom from Alaska for safe keeping before he got killed. What's more, I've been able to translate most of it. And your friend Haskins gets quite a mention.'

11
Outlaw

'I don't want to be a nuisance, Rosa,' Lu Christmas said after taking the vile-tasting medicine Doc Peebles had prescribed. 'I cannot intrude in your life this way. There is a little money left in a bank in Santa Fe. If I can send for it, I will find somewhere else to go. The south of Arizona is said to be good for the lungs – dry and clear.'

Rosa sighed. 'Lu, you're not fit to travel very far. I don't know where you could go, so it's best if you just stay here for the time being.'

Lu's eyes filled but her voice was steady when she thanked Rosa, adding, 'Where is Chad?'

'Oh, he's busy right now – reading some notes I made for him.'

Cooper was in Rosa's office, seated at her small desk, reading her translation of Peter Gilbert's notebook. Rosa hadn't made a full translation, unable in some parts to work out Gilbert's corrupted shorthand, so

123

she had made educated guesses which in most cases seemed to make sense.

Apparently, Gilbert was working on a series of articles about Western outlaws who had managed to escape the law in one way or another. He had several articles already prepared for *Harper's* but the one he was most interested in was about the vicious train-robber known as Larry Bergen. This man had somehow managed to thumb his nose at the law over the years, hiring sharp lawyers to have charges against him dismissed, twice escaping custody and using blackmail and intimidation against judges and witnesses.

Bergen had disappeared almost two years ago. It was claimed he had been killed in a stagecoach accident on the high trail through the Medicine Bow range in Wyoming, his usual stamping-ground.

But Gilbert believed the stagecoach accident had been deliberately set up for the sole purpose of 'killing off' Larry Bergen; the other innocent passengers, driver and guard, had been cold-bloodedly sacrificed for this purpose.

Gilbert was a top investigator in his field, and learned that Bergen was still alive and, using the name of 'Trader Haskins', had become a businessman who was now quite well respected in the southwest. One of Gilbert's contacts had warned him that 'Haskins' had learned of his discovery, and for his own safety, Pete Gilbert accepted an assignment in Alaska, thinking he would be beyond the reach of Bergen. But to be on the safe side, he had sent his notebook to Tom Christmas, an old colleague who knew Gilbert's private shorthand and so could read the notes. Hopefully he could get them published if anything happened to Gilbert.

'Well, something sure did happen to him,' Cooper murmured aloud, as he read the last of the pages written in Rosa's small, neat hand. He glanced up as Rosa entered now, leaving the door ajar. He tapped the page. 'Is this where it ends? I mean, it explains some things, but not what Tom was doing.'

She pulled up a chair beside him, took the small notebook from her apron pocket and opened it at the very last page. It was one of those books that could be slipped into a cover, and replaced with a new one when filled. Cardboard end-pieces slid under the cover's flaps. She took off the leather cover now and on the underside of the back flap showed him a pencilled sketch, presumably drawn by Gilbert.

It took Cooper only a glance to see that it was a very good likeness of 'Trader Haskins', complete with close-cropped beard. Then Rosa took a post-card-size print of the man and woman whom Tom Christmas had asked for. She had sketched in a skimpy, pointed beard on the man's previously clean-shaven face, a match for the one in Gilbert's drawing.

'By God! It's Haskins all right!' exclaimed Cooper.

'Otherwise known as Larry Bergen.'

Cooper scrubbed a hand around his unshaven jowls, flicking his gaze to the girl. She seemed very tight about the mouth, fidgety with her hands. She dropped her eyes and then seemed to decide something and looked at him squarely.

'They were right when they said I had help in

composing and presenting that panorama picture,'
Rosa said quietly.

Cooper started to nod when the door was pushed
open and Lu Christmas came in, holding a small
handkerchief to her mouth. Her almond eyes looked
from one to the other.

'I was not eavesdropping, but I heard what you
said, Rosa. I think you refer to Peter Gilbert?'

Cooper stood and offered her the desk chair, leaning his shoulder against the wall.

Briefly, he told Lu what Rosa had translated so far.

She nodded. 'I know some of this although Tom
would not tell me very much.' She picked up the
postcard and looked at it. She was quiet for a while,
her slim fingers playing with the handkerchief and
when she glanced up again, her eyes were moist. 'My
illness was growing worse. They said I would need an
operation or extended treatment in a St Louis hospi-
tal. We had very little money. Then Tom said he knew
a way to get the money we needed. He would not tell
me any more, but it was soon apparent that he meant
to blackmail this Bergen with the picture. I don't
know how. Then he sent me to St Louis and – and –
I never saw him again.' She saw Cooper's face tighten
and the compressing of his lips. She said kindly, 'You
must not feel guilt about this, Chad. I did not mean
to criticize your part in—'

'Well, that's for me and my conscience, Lu,'
Cooper cut in curtly. 'But we still don't know *why* that
picture is so important – and how Tom knew it was.'
Then he suddenly turned to Rosa. 'You gonna tell us
about Gilbert?'

She nodded. 'I lied when I said I hardly knew him. I have worked on and off with him for years. He started out as a photo-journalist, that is, taking his own pictures to illustrate his articles. As he usually went into the wilds or some dangerous situation, he was in big demand.'

'I remember seeing some of his work – one about Eskimos hunting whales from seal-hide canoes . . .'

'Yes – he liked Alaska. But – we were lovers. It just happened, thrown together by work and so on. He came down here to cover the big Fourth of July celebrations and naturally stayed at my place. I told him about my idea for the panorama picture and he was enthusiastic, keen to try it. So he actually helped me photograph the sections.'

'Including the one with Bergen and the woman,' Cooper dropped in and she nodded.

'Yes. But he was suspicious because the man tried to dodge the camera. Peter waited and caught him unawares. But he didn't give me that photo to include in the panorama, he shot another one, with just the crowd to fit into slot number five.'

'What was the idea of that?'

'He was suspicious of the man, as I said. That sort of thing was enough to set him off, looking into it until his curiosity was satisfied. I don't know what he did but he was sure that the man was Bergen, who had supposedly been killed in a stagecoach accident a couple of years before . . .'

'My God! Keogh told me Bergen had arranged to be held in jail on a pretext that he could be a wanted man. But he needed to get out for a few days early in

July, and didn't want anyone to know he was free at that time. He arranged a stand-in so that Keogh's records would show that Haskins was behind bars right up until the seventh of July. Then Keogh was to release him, claiming it was a case of mistaken identity. Looks like he came here on the fourth of July.'

'But what was so important that he needed such an alibi?' asked Rosa, puzzled. 'It must've been *very* important for him to go to such elaborate lengths! And to get Keogh's co-operation.'

'Well, he had Keogh over a barrel and could force him to do just about anything he wanted . . .'

'As far as I know, Peter never did work it out, but he got word that Bergen was aware of his investigations and that's why he took the Alaska assignment. Was there anything special that happened during the celebration, Chad?'

Cooper frowned, trying to recall the Big Parade as it had become known in Coldwater. It had been a wild time and he had been forced to relax the town laws by order of the council members, because the business section aimed to milk the last cent from visitors who had poured into Coldwater, and they figured the best way to separate these suckers from their money was to give them a couple of days of unrestricted 'fun'. But, by God, Cooper had had his work cut out trying to keep even a semblance of law and order.

There had been brawls, of course, dangerous pranks brought on by drunken bravado, a couple of gunfights, one murder, a drowning in the river, damaged property and a fire in one of the whore-houses. In the end, the town had been mighty glad to allow him to enforce the ordinance – but not before their cash-drawers were full.

'It was a damn wild time,' he said aloud. 'Apart from all the brawls and so on there were a few petty thefts, some horse-stealing and so on, but nothing on a scale that would bring in Bergen and his crew. Damned if I can think of anything that might've drawn a man like Bergen to our town, but obviously there *was* something and until we know what, we're stymied.'

'Bergen and Haskins are the same man,' said Rosa thoughtfully and Cooper agreed with that by a curt nod. 'He would want to make sure as few people as possible knew that, because Bergen was supposed to be dead and as long as the law believed that, he was safe. But that photo could prove he was still alive.'

'Well, it proved there was someone who *looked* like him in Coldwater at that time . . .' Cooper's eyes narrowed. 'But the picture might've been able to be used for blackmail just the same.' He picked up the photograph, tapped it. 'You know, I've seen this woman before. Or maybe I haven't . . . Maybe I've just seen a picture of her, but she looks kind of famil-iar.' He glanced at the women. 'You ever seen her around town, Rosa?'

Rosa shook her head. 'I've studied that print for a long time. I've never seen her before.'

'And Peter sent this picture to Tom, Lu?'

She hesitated, shook her head. 'Not the picture, but the photographic plate.' The almond eyes slid towards Rosa. 'He had you make the picture from it, Rosa.'

She nodded. 'Yes. I knew who had sent Tom the plate, of course, and he admitted it was Peter, but he wouldn't tell me what he was going to do with it.'

'And you worked it all out from the notebook?'

Rosa nodded, looking away quickly.

'Pretty smart work. Or maybe you had a head start.'

Her eyes flashed. 'What d'you mean?'

'Well, you said you and Gilbert were lovers. If he was planning on blackmail, he'd have brought you in on it, I reckon.'

'I didn't want anything to do with it!' she snapped abruptly. 'I thought it was stupid. Writing the articles to expose Bergen was fine, but trying to bleed him of money . . .' She sighed. 'Peter had big ambitions. He was after fame, but only because of the money fame would bring. He was an impatient man in lots of ways and he felt that if he didn't find some short cut it would be too late. He wanted assignments that would allow him to rove the world, not just this country or Mexico. He wanted to take me with him. He never said whether as his wife or – companion. I – don't think I would've cared either way, just as long as I was with him.' She went silent for a short time. Her face was taut as she added, 'As soon as he got word that Bergen knew about his investigations, he went to Alaska . . . not just for his own safety, but for mine.'

'Figured to draw them away from you,' Cooper said and she nodded.

'It's the kind of thing he'd do. I think there must

have been attempts on his life that he didn't tell me about and, being Peter, he probably knew it was only a matter of time before Bergen reached him. So, rather than let all his work go to waste, he contacted Tom, knowing he needed money badly to help Lu. According to his notes he was convinced that Tom could write the articles and get them published and the money would help with his expenses. 'He probably didn't even consider that Tom might try to blackmail Haskins, too.'

'It was a foolish risk,' Lu said slowly and quietly, 'but Tom did it – because of me . . .' Her voice trailed off and they were all silent.

'The woman keeps bothering me,' Cooper said finally, studying the photo again. 'I've got a feeling she's the key to this.'

'Suppose there was someone living in Coldwater who knew Bergen was alive?' Rosa theorized. 'Isn't he the kind of cold-blooded killer who would make sure that man never got a chance to tell anyone?'

'More likely send Jay Booker to handle it for him.'

Rosa looked disappointed and nodded reluctantly. 'Ye-es – I suppose you're right, but' – her face brightened – 'there was a murder during the July Fourth celebration, Chad.'

He waved it aside. 'Two trailmen fighting over a whore. One killed the other and hightailed it. There's still a dodger out on him.'

'Oh. Well, what about the dead man found floating in the river? You said his death was "suspect"?'

He frowned. 'Rudy Swann . . . that feller who was trying to set up a saddlery business. He was pretty badly busted-up. Could've been from washing against rocks in the river or he might've been beaten before being thrown in. Never did get it worked out properly. One of those things you have to end up giving the benefit of the doubt. Even the insurance feller was tossing a coin. Dunno if he ever told the wife she could collect or . . .'

Cooper broke off suddenly, snatched up the picture and stared at it hard.

'That's it. That's where I saw her picture!' He looked at both women. 'This feller from some St Louis insurance company turned up and asked for all details about Swann's death. Wanted to know if it was all above board, or if there were suspicious circumstances, that kind of thing. I told him how I saw it and he showed me a picture of this woman.' He tapped the photo Tom Christmas had had Rosa print. 'Said she was Swann's wife and had put in a claim for a big insurance policy on his life. Said she came from Tucson. They had to be sure everything was legal and the company had sent him down to check. Asked me did I know her or had I seen her around town before or after Swann was killed.'

'What're you saying, Chad?'

'Not sure. But this is the woman, all right. And she's with Bergen in this picture. There's gotta be something to it, the two of them together at that time.'

Before Rosa could answer there was a hammering at the door. she hurried through to see who it was. She came back with the breathless Feeney, hat in hand.

'They're here, Coop – them three fellers you told me to look out for – and they're askin' around for you – an' her.'

He jerked his head towards the suddenly pale Lu Christmas.

'And they look mean as panther's piss – pardon me, ladies ... I was you, Coop, I'd hightail it. Pronto.'

Doc Peebles was leery of the three red-eyed, trail-stained men when they came into his infirmary.

The part-time nurse came running after them, telling them they couldn't go in there, but Jay Booker turned to her, took her by the shoulders, spun her about-face and whapped her a stinging blow across the buttocks, pushing her through the doorway, back into the waiting area.

'Go roll some bandages or somethin',' he grated. 'An' don't poke your head back in here unless you want it knocked off.'

The frightened woman stumbled and put a shaking hand to her mouth as the door closed firmly behind the long-haired killer. Oh, how she wished Chad Cooper was still sheriff! *He* would soon put these roughnecks in their place!

In the infirmary section, Peebles straightened from dressing a wound on a man at the far end of the room and watched Trader Haskins and his two gunmen walk down towards him. From three beds away, the battered, wired-up Cy Maloney watched also, silently, eyes narrowed, wondering who these hardcases were and what they could want here.

'Trader Haskins, Doc.' The man thrust out his hand as he grinned amiably and Peebles found himself automatically joining grips with the hand. 'Sorry to bust in like this but we're on rather urgent business . . .'

Peebles ran his eyes over Lew and Jay Booker. 'You and your friends don't appear to be injured, Mr Haskins.'

'Call me "Trader". No. I'll come right to the point. We've had a long, rough ride down from Santa Fe; before that we came from St Louis . . .'

'A far piece, I venture to say,' Peebles said slyly.

Haskins's grin faded a little and his bad eyes narrowed, not sure if this backwoods sawbones was ribbing him.

'Yes, a far piece indeed, Doctor. We were trying to catch up with a couple of friends of ours, Chad Cooper who was once sheriff here, I believe, and his Chinee friend, a woman named Lu Christmas, if you will believe it . . .'

'Oh, yes, I know Mrs Christmas – and Cooper. But I'm afraid I haven't seen either of them lately.'

Haskins's face straightened out now as he frowned. 'Oh? We checked at the stage depot and they told us that both arrived some hours ago and that the woman was poorly, bad cough and so on. The clerk believed Cooper was going to take her to a doctor . . .'

'There are two of us in town,' Peebles pointed out, and Haskins nodded.

'We've already tried the other man. He was dead drunk and had been that way for three days according to his woman. So that only leaves you, Doc.'

Peebles shook his head, looking helpless. 'Perhaps Cooper changed his mind . . .'

'I shouldn't think so . . .'

'They was here.'

The three killers and Peebles looked towards Cy Maloney's bed as the man ground out the words through his wired-up jaws. Booker strode across.

'What was that, feller?'

Cy watched him with his bruised eyes and spoke again, the words difficult to make out at first but Booker began to decipher them quickly enough. He straightened and looked at Peebles who was trying to remain casual, but his fidgeting hands gave him away.

'This one says Cooper and the Chink were here. Twice. After they come in off the stage, and not long ago when they picked up some medicine for the woman because they was leavin' town. Seems to me your memory's failin', Doc.'

Peebles said nothing now as Deke and Booker ranged themselves alongside him. Haskins sighed, shaking his head slowly.

'Now, that's not friendly, Doc, telling us a pack of lies when we was trying to be polite.'

'I think your friend's right. My memory, must be failing. Because I don't recall Chad Cooper or Lu Christmas being here.' Peebles gestured towards Maloney. 'This man had an anaesthetic not long ago while I reset his busted leg. I believe he's still hallucinating . . .'

'*No!*' grated Maloney and *that* word was clear enough. 'They – was – here!'

Haskins smiled coldly. 'Somehow, Doc, I believe

your patient. Now, s'pose you tell us where Cooper's gone?'

Peebles was silent and then Booker grabbed his right hand and twisted it up his back, bringing the man up to his toes, gasping. 'I – don't – know!'

'All right, Jay – break one of his fingers. If that don't work, stomp on his hand. And if *that* don't work, well, he's got another one . . .' Haskins leaned forward, grinning tightly. 'Reckon you could carry on with *two* busted hands, Doc? One would be bad enough, but . . .'

'*Wait*! I'm telling the truth. Coop never said where he was going. Ask Maloney! He was listening in.'

He glared at Maloney and Haskins asked, 'Doc speaking gospel?'

Cy Maloney hesitated, then nodded. 'Coop never said. But I can tell you where he's likely gone. There's an old gold-mine up in the Coffeepots where he used to go sometimes and scratch around for any nuggets they might've missed . . .'

'You can tell us how to get there?'

Maloney would have grinned viciously if his damaged jaw would have let him, but his eyes glittered, as he nodded.

'You're a vindictive son of a bitch, Cy!' Doc Peebles snapped and Haskins glanced at Booker.

'Stomp on his hand anyway, teach him a lesson.'

Doc yelled as they flung him face down on the floor.

12
Devil's Own

It was a long, hard climb into the Coffeepots to reach the abandoned mine known as Devil's Own.

Cooper had come across it one time after chasing a couple of wild-ass cowpokes out of Coldwater and one of them had shot his horse out from under him, putting him afoot in these mountain lion-ridden ranges. They figured it was a good joke, appeared on a high trail, mocking him, throwing rocks down at him. Until he lifted his salvaged rifle and shot one man, knocking him tail-over-tip so that he dangled over the trail edge. His partner, afraid to expose himself to Cooper's fire, had run off. The man had managed to struggle back and get into his saddle and Coop had hurried him along with a couple of shots over his head. He figured neither man would show his face around Coldwater again.

Then the first mountain lion tried for him in the late afternoon, while he was resting-up in the shade, waiting for the cool of night before travelling on down the long trail to Coldwater. The cougar had made the mistake of thinking he was dead or injured. He shot it in mid-leap and got out of there fast.

He climbed a ridge he had originally aimed to skirt, working in dim starlight before moon rise. It led him to the stark, silent buildings of the Devil's Own and he had spent the night there in the old manager's office, sharing it with a couple of fist-size tarantulas; three packrats and what appeared to be a sick rattler that had had a chunk bitten or torn or shot out of its body. He put it out of its misery and cooked it over a fire outside. While raking through the coals before pushing on he had seen something glittering, picked it up.

A thumbnail-size gold nugget. He took a 'quick' look-around – which lasted most of the day, much to his surprise – and he found three more bits of gold, smaller, but mostly pure. When he got back to town he had them appraised and collected twenty-three dollars for them.

When he had days off – there wasn't a hell of a lot to do or see around Coldwater – he would ride up here and bring a dishpan and pick and shovel. He dug around the ore-heaps and built himself a crude rocker for separating gravel from gold and found, over several weeks, a hundred dollars' worth. There was an old explosives shed with boxes of nitro-oozing dynamite and he risked a few sticks to blow down the abandoned working face, but collected only a few pieces of gold-bearing quartz.

He knew he'd never grow rich but he enjoyed the sense of being on a hunt and he renovated the tumbledown manager's office, put in a crude sapling-

and-gunnysack bunk and a packing-case table with a couple of old oil-lamps he had found and fixed up to working standard.

He didn't came here regularly, but it was a good place to get away to after some hard chores down in town. Coop hadn't made a habit of telling folk about the Devil's Own, but he had had to tell the council members in case he was wanted urgently. He never had been.

Now he took the exhausted Lu into the office he had renovated, kicked out another packrat and had her lie down on the bunk while he used a switch-broom he had made to sweep out most of the dust and animal droppings. Then, following Doc Peeble's directions, he gave her some of the cough medicine, boiled some water on the rust-streaked potbelly stove and poured some into a dish, adding a mixture of pine-oil and menthol supplied by Peebles. Lu draped a towel around her head and leaned her face down into the aromatic steam. She hawked and coughed and gasped, tears streaming down her face.

Afterwards, she seemed weak and pale and was glad to lie down on the bunk. He had coffee made by that time and she wrapped shaking hands around the mug he handed her, sipping gratefully. Her almond eyes sought his face.

'You are a kind man, Chad Cooper.'

He grinned, a mite embarrassed. 'Just caught me on a good day,' he said roughly. 'I better collect more firewood. Gets cool in these mountains at night this time of year.'

She watched him take a rust-flecked tomahawk from where he had jammed the blade between a clapboard and an upright timber and then go out into the late afternoon. She lay back on the bunk and was asleep in minutes.

Trader Haskins and his men were lost in the Coffeepots. They weren't the first and wouldn't be the last victims of their own over-confidence.

They had taken the wrong fork where a trail left a narrow snaking canyon. Maloney hadn't said 'right' or 'left', he had said 'Be sure to take the north fork'. But they had been turned around in their heads by the twisting and turning of the canyon, known as Wriggling Snake to locals, so that they weren't sure of their direction and could not see the sun above the high, narrow walls.

By the time they realized that they must have taken the wrong trail, it was almost dark. Haskins swore viciously but said they might as well make camp for the night.

They were preparing to build a cooking-fire when Deke, who'd been gathering kindling out near the rim of the ledge came running back, excited.

'Trader! I heard someone usin' an axe on the next mountain!'

They all heard it when they went down to the rim: faint but regular thuds, the unmistakable sound of an axe blade biting into wood.

Haskins raised his field-glasses, swept the far slopes which were darkening fast as the sun slid down behind the Coffeepots. 'Can't see anything. Wait!

Just above that little spur over there, I can make out a roofline. Must be one of the mine's buildings. Let's go! It'll be dark before we get there but that'll be to our advantage.'

Lu's cough was bad, relieved some by the inhalation, but she was obviously in pain and she wheezed like a leaky old bellows. Cooper figured there was only one thing for it.

He built up the fire in the potbelly stove, letting it draw until the flames licked up around the hotplate on top. He kept thrusting in more and more wood until the metal began to glow cherry-red. By that time he was stripped to the waist, sixgun rig on an upturned box, with shirt and jacket. Lu seemed to be delirious with a fever and she lay there with the lids of her almond-shaped eyes only half closed. Sweat beaded her face and ran in runnels down her slim neck, soaking the high collar of her *cheong-sam*.

Cooper uncorked the bottle of camphorated oil given to him by Doc Peebles, standing it on a riverstone beside the stove as the woman tossed and turned. The whole inside of the cabin was like an oven and he tied a neckerchief around his head to keep the sweat from running into his eyes.

Now came the part that bothered him a little. But he had let her husband get killed and he wasn't about to let any harm come to Lu Christmas, no matter what.

He began to unbutton Lu's dress from the throat down the front. She murmured and lifted a butterfly-light hand weakly, trying to push him away.

'No,' she murmured, head rolling on the damp pillow.

'Doctor's orders, Lu,' Cooper said tightly, got the dress open to her waist, hesitated briefly, then pulled it wide, pushing it down over her ivory, bony shoulders. Her eyes flew wide and her fingernails raked feebly at his eyes but he got his head aside quickly. It was her only gesture of resistance: she was too weak for more.

He picked up the bottle of oil; the glass was hot, the contents warm as he poured some into the palm of his cupped left hand. He rubbed his hands together to smear the oil over them and then began to massage her ribcage and her chest between her small breasts. She moaned and muttered in her own language, her eyes open now but dulled with sickness and fever. The stench of the evaporating camphor made Cooper turn his head, his eyes watering.

He continued massaging. Then a spasm wracked her and he held her over the side of the bed as she coughed up infected sputum into an old tin he had placed there for the purpose. She lay back, spent, gasping, but the wheezing had eased. He poured more warm oil onto his hands and began the massage again. . . .

She had just finished a second spasm and he was easing her back on to the sweat-soaked bed when the door crashed open and a mocking voice said,

'The hell's this? Some fancy Chink way of whoring?'

Cooper spun, letting Lu drop on to the bunk. He lunged for the box where his sixgun was out of sight beneath his shirt and jacket. Jay Booker took two lunging steps into the heated cabin and tripped him, kicking Cooper hard between the shoulders, then placed a boot across his neck, putting on considerable pressure.

'Don't kill him yet, Jay,' Trader Haskins said. He came inside with Deke, who remained standing by the open doorway, complaining about the furnace heat.

'We seen streams of sparks from half a mile away comin' out of the chimney! What're you playin' at?'

At a sign from Haskins, Booker removed his boot and Cooper sat up, coughing, massaging his bruised and scraped throat.

'The woman's sick,' he grated out and nodded towards the bed as Lu fumbled to pull her bodice closed over her oil-gleaming breasts.

'Not all that sick,' Haskins said with a leer.

'It wasn't like that. I was rubbing camphorated oil into her chest. Can't you smell it?'

'Never mind what I can smell.' Haskins had opened his jacket and loosened his shirt collar. Jay Booker was mopping at his face.

'Let's take 'em outside before we cook, Trader,' he said.

'You'll kill her!' Cooper said quickly, stumbling to his feet, hands half lifted out from his sides as Booker turned a gun in his direction. 'She'll get pneumonia. Can't you close the door?'

'All right. Deke, you stand watch outside but leave the door a little ajar . . .'

Haskins looked at the woman as he gave the order,

then flicked his gaze to Cooper.

'Don't matter to me whether she dies from pneumonia or lead-poisoning – nor you, either. Just hand over those pictures and anything else Gilbert sent Tom Christmas and I'll guarantee you both a quick death.'

'Some deal!'

Haskins spread his hands, smiling, but his eyes were mean and deadly. 'Best you're gonna get, Cooper.' He turned to Jay Booker. 'Jay, that stove's really glowing. Why don't you see what the hot metal can do to Chinee skin while Cooper's deciding how soon he's gonna give me what I want?'

Lu screamed feebly as Booker dragged her roughly from the bunk and pulled her towards the red-hot stove.

'We don't have the pictures!' Cooper said quickly.

'Well, just tell me where I can find them – I'll settle for that. Of course, we're likely to leave you hanging by your thumbs until we go check out your story, or maybe the gal can swing by that long hair . . . So what's it gonna be. . . ?'

'Everything's back in Coldwater.'

Booker had forced Lu to her knees in front of the stove and twisted his hand in her long, jet-black tresses, pushing her face towards the heat-pulsing metal. She made animal moaning sounds that seemed to excite Booker; his eyes glistened, his nostrils flared and his lips drew back tightly across his big teeth.

'Leave her be, goddamnit!' gritted Cooper but Haskins hit him lightly with his gun barrel and he went down on to one knee, shaking his head.

'All right, Jay! Cook her face! *Where* in Coldwater?'

Before Cooper could give any kind of an answer the door crashed open and Deke staggered in, wild-eyed.

'Trader! The brush is on fire and a shed is blazin' like a piece of hell! Them sparks musta set it off!'

'Let it burn . . .' growled Haskins, nodding at Booker who had paused with Lu's face bare inches from the hot metal.

Then Deke added in a choked voice, 'There's a sign on it – says *explosives*!'

'Judas priest!' breathed Cooper, looking truly alarmed. 'There're cases of old dynamite in there! All of 'em sweating nitro—'

'He's lyin'!' Booker said tightly and exerted more effort, surprised at how well the Chinese woman could resist him.

'We've gotta get out of here!' shouted Cooper lunging for the door, but Haskins was too quick, hit him on the back of the head with his gun-barrel and Cooper sprawled, half unconscious, on the floor.

'I'm goin', Trader!' yelled Deke, turning away from the cabin; then he yelled, 'The hosses! The fire's spookin' 'em! Christ! We're gonna lose 'em!'

That was enough for Haskins and Booker. The latter flung the frail woman to the floor and ran for the door. Haskins paused only long enough to make sure Cooper wasn't going anywhere, then followed Booker outside, closing the cabin door behind him.

None of the killers wanted to be stranded in the mountains without horses – they had heard mountain lions coughing and snarling all the way up there.

As the door crashed closed, the rear one opened and Rosa Cisco stepped quickly inside, dressed in jodhpurs, blouse and boots, a hat hanging by its thong down her back. Her face and hands were smeared with soot.

'Quick! I've got your mounts waiting out the back. That dynamite will go at any second!'

Cooper lurched up, blinking, grabbed Lu under one arm and scooped up his shirt, jacket and gunbelt with the other and staggered after Rosa.

Just as they reached the horses, there was an ear-shattering explosion and part of the roof lifted off the cabin. One wall collapsed and the red-hot stove rolled out of the wreckage, scattering its blazing contents across the slope, leaving a trail of flames in its wake.

In minutes the mountain was on fire.

13
Smoke & Gunsmoke

There hadn't been any worthwhile rain for weeks and flames streaked up the trunks of desiccated trees, *whooshing* through the foliage and leaping on to the next tree. The brush on the hillside went up in a crackling burst, flames dancing and leaping wildly, pushing the smoke into grotesque shapes.

Lu had to be roped on to her horse and even then she almost fell. Cooper, still stripped to the waist, sitting on his shirt and jacket, sixgun now buckled about his waist, rode in close and steadied her as best he could. Rosa led the way in the flickering firelight as they raced the flames down the slope.

But it was the slope on the far side, the mountain was now between them and Coldwater. The fire was driving them deeper into the Coffeepots and Cooper knew enough about the area to realize it was going to be a long, dangerous trail back to town.

For one thing, Haskins and his men were also going to be between them and Coldwater. That was if any of them had survived the explosion.

It would be nice to believe that Haskins and Booker and Deke *had* died in the explosion, but Cooper knew better than to put much faith in that kind of vague hope.

For now, all they could do was try to outrun the fire and smoke – which wouldn't do Lu's lungs much good – and then make their way back to Coldwater, and be prepared for ambush every foot of the way.

Actually, Deke was the only one of the killers who was killed in the explosion.

His mount had been badly spooked; he had managed to catch it by the reins but the frightened animal had rolled its eyes, jerked its head and lost its footing. Still clinging to the reins Deke was dragged across the slope by the racing horse and, in panic, released his hold.

He would have done better to keep gripping the reins.

He fell and rolled, out of control, down the steepest part of the slope – towards the blazing explosives shack, screaming all the way. But the scream was soon lost in the blast of the explosion which sent a wall of flame and debris hurtling across the mountain.

Somewhere in the midst of it was what was left of Deke. It wasn't much.

Haskins and Booker were knocked flat by the blast, their horses shrieking and plunging. Both men managed to hang on to the bridles although they had a mighty rough time of it. Then, ears ringing, bodies battered, sore and aching, they realized they had survived.

'Jeeeeesussss!' exclaimed Booker, blowing out his cheeks as he jammed a finger into one ear, working at the dizzy buzzing inside his head. '*Whaooeee*! Now that was some Fourth of Ju-ly!'

Haskins scowled, head spinning, legs weak as he fought to get into the saddle. Booker, staggering, clawed his way aboard his prancing horse.

'Man, that's one helluva fire!'

'There're still a few patches not burning yet – we can get across if we hurry.'

'Reckon that blast finished Cooper and the Chink gal?'

Riding for parts of the brush that were not yet ablaze, Haskins glanced up towards the shattered cabin where Cooper and Lu had been.

He didn't answer but his face looked grimly uncertain. He wouldn't be happy until he saw the bodies.

Cooper and the two women found shelter amongst rocks in an unexpected boulder-field almost at the base of the mountain. Vegetation was sparse and the huge rocks were tumbled about in wild confusion, like massive marbles some giant had spilled.

There wasn't a real cave, but there were pockets here and there with boulders weighing many tons jammed a few feet above the ground between other great rocks. So they stopped in one of these, laying Lu on the coarse grit of the cleared ground.

'You – go on,' she said weakly. 'I'll be all right

here. You can come back for me later – they won't
find me.'

'We're not leaving you, Lu,' Cooper said, finality
in his voice, taking time now to put on his shirt, for it
was cold. But he draped his jacket over Lu. He
glanced at Rosa. 'Glad you showed when you did . . .'

'I remembered you telling me about the Devil's
Own. I saw Haskins and his men moving in and then
the sparks flying out of the stove's chimney gave me
an idea when I saw that some had started small fires
on the slope. So I started one of my own. Behind the
explosives shed . . '

'Well, it all worked out. I just hope the blast killed
Haskins. What brought you up here, though?'

Rosa settled herself as comfortably as she could,
fussing. She didn't seem to want to look directly at
Cooper.

She said, quietly, 'I felt bad about lying to you
about Peter and so on. Can't help thinking that if I
hadn't, some people might still be alive.'

He knew she likely meant Hank Keogh and
Lonnie – it had already been too late for Tom
Christmas. Her worried glance in Lu's direction told
him she was concerned for her, too – afraid she
wouldn't live through this ordeal. So she had come
to do what she could. Typical of Rosa, he thought,
but kind of pointless, too, although he and Lu owed
their lives to her.

The Chinese woman had drifted into sleep but she
stirred slightly now and Cooper scrubbed a hand
down his grimy face, squeezing some of the weariness
from his eyes. He picked up his rifle and grunted as

he heaved to his feet, though forced to stoop over because of the overhanging rock.

'I'd better keep look-out just in case that dynamite didn't finish Haskins and his crew,' he said, moving away as he stifled a yawn.

The morning smelled strongly of smoke: burned-out timber and raw smoke that hacked at a man's throat as it rolled across the blackened slopes in the chill early breeze.

The cold brought Cooper jarring awake and he snatched at his rifle, which had slipped from his grip during the night. The metal was icy against his fingers.

He eased himself between the boulders and looked up the slopes, heart pounding, cursing himself for having slept. It was a scene of desolation, like the aftermath of the summer forest-fires that were more or less a regular feature of the Coffeepots. What timber was left standing was blackened and still smouldering. Smoke hung over the mountain like a fog. Other trees had fallen and burned away to piles of grey and black ash, some still with a red glowing heart.

But he couldn't see any movement up there. No animals, no riders! *Well, thank you God!* he thought. It looked as if Haskins had been killed in the blast after all.

He had had to find a path through a tangled maze of boulders in the dark. Now he made his way back in the dim, grey light of early morning. It would be brighter as the sun rose higher, but still it confused him. He knew he had taken a wrong turning; as he backed up he heard Lu's coughing well over to his left instead of straight ahead. He turned up a narrow path towards the sound, down on hands and knees, and suddenly found himself in familiar territory. He scrabbled his way through and came out to the place where Rosa and the Chinese woman waited.

Only thing was, they had company.

Haskins and Jay Booker, the latter sitting with the weakened, coughing Lu between his straightened legs as he lounged back against a boulder at his ease. He had one arm about her slim waist and the other hand held his sixgun pressed lightly into her side.

Haskins, smiling coldly, sat opposite Rosa, covering her with his Smith & Wesson.

'Come join us, Cooper,' he invited. 'We almost missed you. If it hadn't been for our little Chinee here, giving us a cough or two, we'd have ridden right on by. But I guess the stink of that camphor would've led us to her anyway.'

'I am sorry, Chad!' sobbed Lu but he smiled faintly and lifted a hand.

'Can't be helped, Lu.' He looked at the two men. 'Well, Haskins? Or Bergen, or whatever you want to call yourself – I don't suppose you want to satisfy our curiosity before you kill us?'

'Hell, no. Why would I do that?' Haskins grinned tightly, in control now. 'Got you stymied, eh?'

'Not sure. My guess is you murdered Rudy Swann and made it look like a drowning accident. That picture could put you on the spot, even though you'd arranged what you figured as a foolproof alibi through Keogh.'

Haskins was sober now. 'Why would I want to kill this Rudy Swann? Whoever he was . . .'

'He could identify you – but you were supposed to be dead. And then there was the insurance . . .'

It was a stab in the dark but it went straight to the bullseye.

'Judas, Trader, he knows more'n we figured.'

Haskins glared at Booker. 'Shut up, Jay!' Then he turned his hard eyes on to Cooper. 'You're guessing.'

'But it's a pretty good guess, isn't it?'

Suddenly Haskins smiled crookedly and nodded. 'Well, you're right, Cooper. But not all the way right.'

Cooper nodded. 'No. The rest has something to do with the woman, doesn't it?'

Haskins stiffened at his words, then laughed, a touch of bitterness in the sound. 'You son of a bitch! You got me talking about it, after all, didn't you? Well, you know nearly all, I might as well give you the rest now. The woman was Ida Swann, Rudy's wife.'

Cooper stiffened and looked quickly at Rosa. 'We kind of fingured that . . . She hire you to kill her husband?'

'Damn near had it figured, didn't you?' Haskins said, not quite so smug now. 'Like me, she was s'posed to be somewheres else, a long way from Coldwater – Tucson, in her case. See, we knew each other long before she married Rudy. We – kept in touch, you might say, and Rudy caught us one time. Which is why he got pissed at her and threatened to go to the marshals and tell them that I was still alive.

But he didn't know what name I was using at the time and when Ida got word to me I went to ground for a spell. He got scared and hightailed it. Took us a long time to track him down to Coldwater. By that time he was talkin' divorce, lookin' for an easy way out, or trying to save face, I dunno.'

'He knew you'd kill him to make sure he kept his mouth shut,' put in Cooper quietly.

Haskins sneered. 'Yeller bastard! He never bitched when he collected his pay-offs. Ida worried him though, said if he went to the marshals, he'd be in trouble himself. So that's when he ran, and got this idea of the divorce. Not sure what he had in mind, but he never reckoned with Ida. For years she'd been payin' premiums on an insurance policy she sweet-talked him into takin' out when they was first married. She must've had some plans about it even then. He never even remembered it, but she kept up the payments and figured if Rudy had to die anyway, she wanted the insurance money – which wouldn't be paid to her if he was murdered or committed suicide, or they'd been divorced. So we had to figure somethin' out to make it look like a natural death.'

'Sounds like you make a good pair.'

Haskins chuckled. 'You dunno just *how* good, Cooper! Anyway, we had word he was hidin' out down here and then Coldwater put on that big Fourth of July parade. Suited us fine – lots of people coming and going, hundreds of strangers in town, plenty of wild times goin' on . . .' He shrugged, spread his hands. 'A man could disappear and no one'd even notice. Was Ida come up with the idea of

drownin' him in the river. No hassle at all to drag
Rudy away one night, give him a beatin' to let him
see he wasn't gonna get away with threatenin' me.
Then we dumped him in the river – Ida said any
marks on him would be put down to the currents
bangin' him against rocks and so on. And that's just
what you thought, wasn't it, Cooper?' Haskins
grinned. 'Now they're gonna pay the insurance
money to Ida and we're gonna live happily ever after.
Ain't that a pretty endin'?'

'Well, looks like you made it, Bergen,' Cooper said
quietly, stalling, looking for an opening that might
give them a chance. 'You got us all, the woman and
the money . . .'

'Guess I always was lucky,' Haskins smirked.

'But you don't have the original plates of the
picture or the research that Pete Gilbert had done
on you,' said Rosa tautly.

That wiped the smirk off Haskins's face. 'But I got
you, sweetheart. Maybe that's even better.'

She shook her head. 'Those papers and the photographic plates are where you'll never get your hands
on them. And if I don't return to Coldwater,
unharmed, by a certain time, they'll go straight to
the federal marshals – so maybe you haven't really
won at all.'

Haskins slapped her across the face, swung the
Smith & Wesson back swiftly, and poked it into
Cooper's face as the man started to get up. 'Whatever
happens, you ain't gonna know about it, sweetheart!
None of you are! I've had a bellyful and I'll take my
chances with the marshals.' He grinned crookedly.

'My guess is you left the papers with some attorney in Coldwater. How many can there be in a dump like that, eh?' He laughed as Rosa paled. 'Won't take me ten minutes to locate the right one. Meantime, you're all dead – right here. Right – *now*!' He nodded to Booker.

But Cooper was ready for it, ducked under the big Smith & Wesson as it fired and the ricocheting bullet disconcerted Haskins and Booker for a moment. Then Lu came to life and rammed backwards with her bony elbow, right into Booker's crotch. The man sagged sickly, groaning, and the slim, ailing Chinese woman turned on him and raked his face with her nails, ripping the corner of one eye, shredding his cheek – screaming at him in her own language. Cooper didn't savvy a word but figured it would have something to do with Booker having been the one to murder Tom in cold blood.

Booker struck out, hitting her, knocking her sprawling. Rosa threw herself across Lu and Cooper kicked Haskins in the face. The man reeled, slipped and slid awkwardly over a rock, palmed up his Colt and triggered. The twin shots from Cooper's Colt bloomed through the rocks like thunder. There was no ricochet this time: both bullets drove into Haskins's chest smashing him to his knees. Sobbing, he tried to raise his smoking gun but was knocked flat by Cooper's third slug.

Booker was crawling away under the rocks, one hand pressing into his aching groin, only wanting to get out into the open where he could drag down a long gulp of fresh air. Cooper saw that the women were unharmed and lunged after Booker.

The killer was waiting for him, kneeling beside a rock, steadying himself with his left hand while he lifted his gun with his right, teeth bared against the knifing pain in his guts. Cooper dived headlong through the opening, spraying sand and gravel as he landed, firing wildly. The bullet ricocheted in a cloud of dust from the rock beside Booker's hand and the man triggered, but his shot was way off. With a roar, he heaved to his feet and swaying, limping, lurched towards Cooper, gun held out in front of him in both hands, thumbing the hammer.

Cooper dropped flat, spun away, rose to his knees, his Colt's barrel angled up, and put his last two shots into Booker's face. The man was flung almost completely over a boulder which darkened with his blood as his limp body hung there. Cooper was on his feet when Rosa came out, supporting Lu.

'All right?' he asked Lu and she nodded, smiling faintly.

'I feel better now,' she said, looking at the dead gunman.

'Me, too,' Cooper agreed flatly. 'Now that it's nearly over.'

Rosa was sober, her eyes steady an Cooper's face.

'Nearly? You're thinking of Rudy's wife. . . ?'

'She's a murderer, too.'

'You're going to Tucson, aren't you?' Rosa sounded slightly breathless.

He shrugged. 'Everyone seems to want me out of town. Might as well head south as any other direction.'

Rosa drew in a deep breath, her gaze unwavering. 'Not . . . everyone wants you to go, Chad,' she said quietly.

He smiled faintly. 'In that case, maybe I'll come back . . .'

She watched his face soberly. 'You can't really prove Ida Swann had anything to with Rudy's death. It's only Haskins's word . . .'

'*I* know she did it . . . motivated by greed.'

'Chad – you – what're you going to do?' There was a catch in her voice, as if she was afraid to hear his answer.

But he only met and held her gaze, not speaking.

Then Lu said huskily, 'She deserves to die. A woman who would help plan the death of her own husband . . .' She shook her head, lips tightening, showing no compassion.

'Lu's right,' Cooper allowed quietly. He knew she savvied what had to be done.

Rosa frowned. 'But Chad – a – woman!'

'A *killer*, Rosa. And she helped murder Swann while I was sheriff.'

'That's it, isn't it? It happened while *you* were lawman! A blow to your pride . . .'

'Just shows I didn't do my job as well as I should've.' His words were clipped, his face unrelenting.

Rosa's eyes filled with tears, her voice trembled. 'Chad – you should leave it to the law!' He said nothing and she added quietly, 'It – it might not be worth your while to come back to Coldwater if you go through with this your way, Chad.'

'Only way I know,' he said. The silence dragged on, then he heaved a sigh, glanced at Lu who kept her face carefully neutral. Then he nodded shortly, face hard.

'Well, that's the way life goes sometimes, I guess. You win some, you lose some.'

He turned abruptly and went to gather up the horses for the long ride back to town.